$4.00

ALIENS!

Other GRUBSTAKE ADVENTURES
by Nathan Aaseng:

Sneak Attack!

Swamped!

THE GRUBSTAKE ADVENTURES

ALIENS!

NATHAN AASENG

Augsburg
MINNEAPOLIS

ALIENS!

Cover art by Dawn Mathers
Interior design by Julie Humiston

Library of Congress Cataloging-in-Publication Data

Aaseng, Nathan.
  Aliens! / Nathan Aaseng.
    p. cm. — (The grubstake adventures series)
  ISBN 0-8066-2838-3 (alk. paper)
  [1. While the whole camp is in turmoil over reports of aliens and escaped convicts, Tony, a dude wrangler, overcomes his inexperience with horses. 2. Camp—Fiction. 3. Horses—Fiction. 4. Christian life—Fiction.] I. Title. II. Series: Grubstake adventures.
PZ7.A13A1 1995   95-286
[Fic]—dc20   CIP
                                                AC

The paper used in this publication meets the minimum requirements of American National Standard for Information Services—Permanence of Paper for Printed Library Materials, ANSI Z329.48-1984.   ∞

Manufactured in the U.S.A.   AF 9-2838

99	98	97	96	95	1	2	3	4	5	6	7	8	9	10

CONTENTS

To Homer Perkins, Doc and Maude

Dude Wranglers

So you're the dude wranglers for the week," said Wrangler Rick as he kicked open the long, rough wooden gate. "You tenderfeet think you can go the distance?"

Tony Schmidt's eyebrows had flown up under his blond bangs at the first sight of Wrangler Rick, and they had not come down yet. "Uh, yeah," Tony said. "Sounds like fun. Don't it, Lamont?"

"It better be," Lamont said. "My parents coughed up big bucks for this week." Lamont was Tony's neighbor and one of the smartest kids in their grade. They usually got along well, and Tony called Lamont his friend, although they did not really hang out together much outside of school.

Rick chuckled. He walked a slow, heavy-legged gait, just like Tony pictured a real cowboy would. Maybe it was the cowboy boots that made them walk like that. "Are you really a cowboy?" Tony asked.

"You mean, do I live out on the range and drive cattle?" Rick asked. "Naw."

"So how do you know so much about horses?" Lamont asked. He sounded as skeptical as Tony felt.

"Been around them most of my life. My dad rode broncos in the rodeo." Rick suddenly stopped and studied Tony's curious expression. He must have found what he was looking for because his dark face broke into a wide grin. "Didn't anybody ever tell you the Wild West had black cowboys?"

Tony blushed until his face almost matched his freckles. Rick knew exactly what he had been thinking. "No, I guess nobody ever did," he said. "I mean, I guess I just wasn't expecting . . . well, you know."

Rick laughed easily, which helped Tony shed some of that painful awkwardness. "Yeah, I know. Lot of people don't know what the real West was like," he said.

Lamont smashed a deerfly that had landed on him. He rolled the fly out of the long, tousled hair on top of his head down to the clean-shaved sidewalls and picked it off. "So when do we start riding?"

"I don't reckon we're going to ride at all today," Rick said. "There's a lot more to wrangling than just sitting on a horse. Right now, you're going to help Miller hitch up the team so we can get all the campers' gear out to the villages."

Anyone who had ever spent time at Camp Horizon, more commonly known as Camp Grubstake, knew Miller the maintenance man. Like most campers, Tony did not know if Miller was the man's first name or last name. Miller's thin, boney features reminded Tony of a scarecrow. Yet he was the sprightliest old man Tony had ever seen. Tony could not remember ever seeing a man Miller's age run. But Miller ran everywhere, one hand holding his straw hat onto his head, the other stiff out to the side. Unless he was leading a horse, as he was doing now. Then he slowed down.

"Come on, Belle. Up now, Governor," Miller said, as he led two large, thick-legged chestnut horses toward a long, green trailer.

"Man, look at the size of those horses!" Tony marveled. "Talk about built for power!" He knew they were the gentlest of animals, yet he felt nervous being so close to anything that could crush him so easily.

"Naw, Clydesdales are stronger," Lamont said.

"Clydesdales are show horses," said Rick. "These are workers. They can outwork any four Clydesdales around. Now you two help out Miller until suppertime. I've got a lot of boring stuff to do, like taking inventory in the stable."

They found Miller hard at work. The team driver never saw them until he finished strapping Belle and Governor into their harnesses. He rushed over to the boys and put a hand on Tony's shoulder while he shook Lamont's hand. "I'm sorry, boys, I didn't see you. Didn't know you were coming so soon." He looked at his watch and grimaced. "Oh, look at the time. I'm sorry I can't let you do much now, but time is slipping away so fast and I have to get out to the villages so the boys and girls have all their belongings. I want them to have a good week here at Camp Horizon.

And I wish the same for you boys, too, you know. But can you help me load up the wagon for now?" Then he dashed back to his work.

Tony and Lamont just shrugged at each other. That was Miller. He did not act or talk like anyone Tony had ever met. But with Miller that was okay. You could not help but like Miller.

They spent the next hour loading sleeping bags, backpacks, duffel bags, and suitcases onto the wagon. Miller placed blocks of wood between piles to distinguish one village's gear from another's.

"This isn't what I signed up for," Lamont grumbled in a low voice. "I want to ride horses, not load luggage."

"Rick says we'll get our chance," said Tony. He tried to act cheerful, sensing that Lamont was still irritated at having been corrected about the Clydesdales. "I don't mind a little work."

Lamont looked at him like he was crazy.

When at last the gear was loaded, the boys hustled up beside Miller who stood holding the reins behind the buckboard of the wagon. As he walked by with the last of the sleeping bags, Tony studied Governor's milky eyes for a moment. He could never get used to the fact that the horse was blind. Somehow that never stopped Governor from pulling the wagon all over Camp Grubstake.

"Belle, Governor," Miller said, quietly. The horses lurched into a brisk walk, catching Tony off guard. He toppled backward. Before he could right himself, he knocked over a tall suitcase and pitched into a pile of sleeping bags.

"Belle, Governor, whoa," said Miller. "Are you hurt, son?"

Tony looked up and saw the wagon driver looking absolutely crestfallen, while Lamont was almost doubled over, stifling laughter. "No, I'm fine."

"Could you hold these?" asked Miller, giving the reins to Lamont, who suddenly looked a little scared. Miller then waded through the gear and helped Tony to his feet. "I surely didn't mean to do that to you. You know, we're going to have to work harder to hold on, or I'm afraid you won't last the week."

"I'll be okay," said Tony. "I just wasn't paying attention."

Miller retook the reins. Tony wanted to forget the embarrassing incident. But between Miller stealing concerned glances at him now and then and Lamont grinning at him, it was not easy. They moved on, clattering up the dirt road toward Valley Village where the younger campers were staying. This was one of two weeks in the summer when Camp Grubstake was open to younger kids as well as middle schoolers and high school students.

They unloaded the gear designated for Valley Village and moved on toward Forest Village. At the top of a short hill, the wide valley closed to a narrow road hemmed in by trees and brush on all sides. The slowly passing leaves and branches, the warm sun, and the steady clop of the horses had a hypnotic effect on Tony. To keep himself alert he studied the woods, looking for birds or squirrels or unusual tree trunks. His eyes settled on a flash of white next to an old hickory stump. Tony wondered if it was a big mushroom or maybe just a sign of some sort.

"Do you see that?" He started to point, when suddenly the white splotch seemed to move. Over the creaking of the wagon and Governor's snorting, Tony heard rustling where the splotch disappeared. His eyes widened. "What is that?" he said.

"What's what? Where?" asked Lamont, craning to see around Miller.

"Over there on the right, by that old stump."

"I heard something scurrying about," said Miller. "I would suppose it was some small animal. You mustn't be afraid, though. There's nothing really dangerous at Camp Grubstake."

"So what did you think you saw—a bear?" Lamont asked, stifling another laugh.

"Well, no. It was, like, bald. Almost like a bald head, I think," said Tony, realizing that his words sounded crazy.

"A bald head. You're sure?" asked Lamont, suddenly interested.

"I don't know," said Tony, shrugging. "It was just a quick flash in woods and a shuffling sound. Hard to know what I saw, it happened so fast." He was willing to let the matter drop.

"Can we stop and take a look?" asked Lamont.

Miller stared at his watch and bit his lip in an expression of profound regret. "Oh, I'm afraid not, boys. I'm already three minutes late. I don't want the children in Forest Village to think they can't rely on me."

"That's okay," said Tony. He stared hard at the woods but saw no further movement. "Ah, who knows. Probably nothing."

"Yeah," chuckled Lamont. "Probably just a bald-headed squirrel. Either that or an alien spy. Nothing to get excited about."

TWO

Alien Sighting

Oooh, I just love horses!" Bridget Korba squealed for at least the fourth time in the past ten minutes.

"How many times do you have to say that?" Juanita de la Rosa complained. "We both like horses. That's why we signed up for this camp, remember?"

"But you're not absolutely, incredibly, hopelessly, fabulously insane about horses like I am!" Bridget insisted.

"I wouldn't go around bragging about it if I was." Juanita looked down at her friend, who was nearly a head shorter. Bridget was always falling off the deep end about something or other. Last spring it had been country western music, of all things. "Why can't we just really like horses and enjoy our week and leave it at that? Why do we have to turn this into some life and death romance?"

"I can't help how I am," said Bridget, sucking on the ends of her hair that constantly fell in her face. "If you don't like me the way I am, you don't have to be my friend."

"Oh, pleeeease," Juanita groaned, wondering if Bridget would survive to adulthood despite having her heart broken every couple of weeks. "Which one do you want to ride?"

All the riding horses stood out in the pasture, heads down as they munched on clover or whatever else they were finding. The sun had set, and in the fading light of the evening they looked almost ghostly.

"ALL OF THEM!" gushed Bridget. "I absolutely have to ride all of them. They're so gorgeous."

"Are you going to ride them all at once or do you think you might try one at a time?" asked Juanita.

"Mmmmmm," said Bridget, as if reading over a dessert menu. "I think I'll take Sheik. He has such a romantic name."

"I'm riding Dusty," Juanita declared. "I don't care about her name. But I rode her last year and she has the smoothest trot. She gives the best rides."

A door creaked open on the converted tobacco-curing shed that served as the horse barn. Wrangler Rick walked out, flanked by his two dude wranglers. "Hey!" said Bridget. "How come those two boys got to go in the barn?"

"They must be in the wrangler program," explained Juanita, adjusting her glasses on her nose. "They get to spend all week with the horses."

"What?" shrieked Bridget. "I would die to do that! How did they get so lucky? Why don't we get to do that?"

"Would you stop screaming?" Juanita said. Bridget was being even worse than usual. Juanita wondered if coming to camp with her was a mistake. "You have to be a year older to be a dude wrangler. We can sign up for that next year."

"That's not fair! They don't look any older than we do."

"Everyone looks older than you," Juanita said with a smile.

"I don't need your short jokes, thank you very much," Bridget said.

Rick and the dude wranglers drew near. Bridget zipped open the money pouch she carried on her waist. "I'll give you ten bucks to trade places with me," she called to the boys, holding up a few bills. "Make that twenty."

"Trade places for what?" asked Tony.

"Let me be the dude wrangler. Please! How about twenty-five?"

"Put your money away, kid," said Wrangler Rick. "I take only two wranglers a week, and I select them in advance. The position's closed."

Bridget latched onto Lamont's arm. "Okay, I'll settle for the next best thing. I'll be your girlfriend for the week."

Lamont stared at her in disbelief. "I have never seen this person before in my entire life," he said to Tony.

"You girls need to get back to your village," Rick reminded them. "Your campfire will be starting any minute."

"We're on our way," Juanita said, grabbing Bridget's arm and prying it loose from Lamont. She had totally lost patience with her friend.

"But it's getting dark," protested Bridget. "We should have an escort or something."

"You've got each other," Rick pointed out.

"And that's just fine," said Juanita, as she pulled her friend down the road.

"I don't know," said Lamont, with mock seriousness. "It may not be safe, what with all these aliens running loose."

"Right! Bridget, move your feet. I'm not going to drag you the whole way," Juanita warned.

"What do you mean, aliens?" asked Bridget, excited.

"Nothing," said Tony.

Lamont grinned. "Hey, it's true. Tony saw a weird, bald-headed thing running around in the woods just before supper."

"You always exaggerate," Tony complained. "I don't really know what it was—if it was anything. I just heard a noise and at a quick glance it looked like something, but it wasn't."

"That's not what he said before," Lamont said, mysteriously. "I'd be careful out there if I were you."

"Lamont!" said Tony.

"Fine. You want to walk back by yourself, go ahead," said Juanita, finally letting go of Bridget's arm.

That did the trick. Seeing her friend disappear into the dusk, Bridget scurried after her. "Wait, I'm coming."

"It's about time," Juanita declared. "So help me, if you're going to pull this kind of stuff all week, I don't even want to be around you. I'll ask for a transfer to another village."

Bridget ignored her. She hovered so close to Juanita that she nearly bumped her off the dirt road and into the bushes. "I don't like walking out here by ourselves," she said. "This is creepy."

"Okay, if you don't like walking, let's run." Juanita took off down the road, hoping there weren't too many ruts in it. She liked running in the dark—it always gave the illusion that she was going twice as fast as she really was. Besides, the faster they got back to Meadow Village, the less she would have to put up with Bridget's fear of the dark.

"Juanita!" screamed Bridget. "Don't you dare leave me." But instead of joining Juanita, she stood still.

"Come on, then. I'm not running fast."

"Juanita!" Bridget stayed rooted to her spot.

Juanita could just make out Bridget's small shadow among the larger shadows of the trees. She stopped. With an exasperated sigh, she turned and waited for her friend. She heard the faint crunching of Bridget's feet on some loose rocks.

Suddenly there was a rustling on the hill to the left of the road. "EEEEEEE!!!!" shrieked Bridget. She took off sprinting straight toward Juanita. As she drew close, Juanita saw the whites of her friend's eyes glowing in the fading dusk light, looking almost as big as hard-boiled eggs.

"Run! Run!" screamed Bridget. "There's something in the woods!"

"What is it?" Juanita called, alarmed. But a further rustling in the deep shadows cut short any further questions. Juanita grabbed Bridget's hand and tore off down the road. She was faster than Bridget and was running faster than she had ever run before. She dragged Bridget along so hard that she nearly pulled her off her feet.

They raced down the trail. Everything was a blur. Juanita searched desperately for lights from the camps farther down the valley. As they rounded a bend, she saw flashlights shining from the left. "Who is it?" she cried, breathlessly.

"Hey, hey, hold on, hold on. It's Poke with some of my mellow campers. What's this all about?"

Juanita felt immediate relief. Poke was one of the veteran counselors at Camp Grubstake. But Bridget was still wound up tight. "Run!" she gasped.

Poke threw an arm out to stop Bridget. Exhausted by her run, Bridget made no further effort to get past her. "Easy now, girls," said Poke. "You're scaring me, here. Let's be cool. What happened?"

With Bridget too winded to talk, Poke looked to Juanita for an explanation. "I don't know," Juanita huffed. "Bridget saw something. Said it was after her."

"Did you see it?" asked Poke.

"No," said Juanita. "She was behind me. I didn't see anything. It was kind of dark. I heard something, though."

Poke clasped Bridget around the shoulders. "You're okay, now. It's all right. You're with friends. Tell me what happened."

Bridget stared up at her, still shaking with fear. "It was horrible!" she said. "I just caught a glimpse of it. I saw these weird, horrible eyes and then it was coming at me!"

"Whoa, what are we talking about? A person, an animal?"

"I don't know," said Bridget. "It seemed like almost both. It was so strange. It was like nothing I ever saw before, like an alien or something."

"Aliens?" laughed some of the voices behind the flashlights.

Juanita turned skeptically toward her friend. She knew that Bridget had been reading books about UFO sightings. That wrangler kid and his talk about aliens just to scare them! Add that to Bridget's hyperactive imagination and a dark trail in the woods, and what do you expect? Sure, now she's seeing aliens! Juanita felt so embarrassed she wanted to hide.

"Hey, now, leave her alone," said Poke to her chuckling campers. "Did you get a good look at this, whatever scared you?"

"I didn't stick around to look," said Bridget. "When I saw these eyes coming out of the woods, I took off."

"Well, it could have been an animal," Poke said, soothingly. "Sometimes a squirrel or a woodchuck or even a deer will catch you off guard. In the dark, you know another pair of eyes can look pretty frightening."

"This didn't seem like any animal," Bridget insisted. "This was so weird."

"Well, you're all right now," said Poke. "If you really want us to, I suppose we could ask Miller or Pat, the camp director, to check on it. But if it was an animal, it's gone by now. Who's your counselor?"

"Shana," Juanita and Bridget said at once.

"Good. Our group is joining you for campfire tonight," said Poke. "Come on with us. And from now on, be sure you carry a flashlight when you're walking around in the dark. You'll feel better."

"I'm not going anywhere in the dark—with or without a flashlight," said Bridget, with a shudder. "From now on, I'm not leaving the village after supper unless it's with the whole group."

As they tagged along with Poke's group, Juanita burned with humiliation. She had let Bridget scare her witless, probably over some dumb chipmunk. She took pride in being tough, and now Poke and her girls probably thought she was a total loon.

"It's all those dumb wrangler boys' fault," Bridget huffed as they stepped into the glow of the Meadow Village fire. "They should have escorted us like I asked."

You got part of that right, Juanita thought. It was the dude wranglers' fault. Aliens, right!

Minds of Their Own

Tony approached the horse barn nervously on Monday morning. He had been up since before dawn, tingling with nervous energy. His excitement over the chance to work with horses had been the dreamy, wishful thinking type. He had thought riding horses would be like a ride at an amusement park—full of thrills and excitement. But yesterday, when he had actually drawn near to a real, living horse, he saw that it was not at all like a roller coaster or a scrambler or a water slide. For all the thrills those rides provided, they were perfectly safe. They would have to be or else the lawyers would never let them stay open to the public.

Horses were different. They weren't safe. They were animals—big animals—and Tony was not used to being around animals. His family did not even own a dog. Horses were powerful creatures that did not always do what you wanted them to. They had minds of their own, and teeth and hooves and legs that could do damage. And saddles had no seatbelts.

Rick's words of warning had added to his skittishness. "Never walk directly behind a horse," he had said. "They don't like people back where they can't see them."

Tony clung to the hope that after spending several days with horses he would start to get used to them—maybe by Tuesday or Wednesday. But in the meantime, he stepped warily around the animals.

Wrangler Rick greeted them at the stable door with a couple of pitchforks. "You're right on time, cowpokes. We'll start you off putting straw in the stalls and hay in the troughs."

"What is this?" griped Lamont. "All we ever do around here is grunt work."

Rick grinned at him. "You think this is bad? I'll bet you have never shoveled out a stable. You have that to look forward to."

"I signed up for this program so I could ride horses," Lamont insisted. "You think you might be able to fit that into the week somehow?"

"Sure thing. You'll start riding this afternoon."

"This afternoon?" squawked Lamont. "What's wrong with this morning? It doesn't take that long to throw straw around a barn."

"No, it doesn't," agreed Rick. "But you'll be pleased to know we have another task to perform. It seems that one of the groups in the Pioneer Village wants to set up camp in the meadow on top of the ridge this week. Pat gave them the go-ahead. So it's our job to pack their gear up by horse."

"More heavy lifting," groused Lamont.

"Can Belle and Governor really pull that wagon up the ridge trail?" asked Tony.

"No, the trail's too steep for a wagon," Rick said. "That's why we're going to saddle pack Socks and Petey and walk them up."

"I quit," muttered Lamont.

"That's fine," Rick said, cheerfully. "I have a long waiting list of applicants to replace you."

"Like your girlfriend for the week," teased Tony.

"Give me a break."

By the time they finished spreading the straw and hay, Tony was exploding with sneezes.

"You got hay fever?" asked Rick.

"I don't know," Tony said, sniffling. His eyes felt itchy and his nose was running. "I've never been around hay before."

"Doesn't look good for a dude wrangler," said Rick. "We may have to keep you away from the hay."

"Did I tell you that I'm allergic to manure?" Lamont said jokingly.

"Nice try," said Rick. "You'll be shoveling along with the rest of us. But for now, let's go fetch the horses."

As they walked out to the pasture, Tony asked, "How do you fetch a horse? What's the trick?"

"Just walk up to the horse, real calm," Rick said. "When you get close, pet him and talk to him nicely. Take hold of his halter. Then lead him into the barn. I've got their names on the stalls so you know where to put them."

Rick approached two horses that looked at him blankly. He rubbed their necks, took the halter, and started walking them to the stable.

Tony and Lamont looked at each other and shrugged. "Nothing to it, I guess," Tony said. But just to be safe, he selected the smallest horse, a brown and white fellow named Oscar, as his target.

"Good morning, Oscar," he said sweetly. Oscar jerked his head up and stared suspiciously at Tony. "Good ol' Oscar," Tony said, slowly stepping toward the horse. Oscar tossed his head and walked away.

"Oscar!" Tony called. "Come on, we're just going to the barn. You've done that a hundred times." Oscar put his head down and walked slowly away from Tony as he munched on grass.

"Problems, Cowboy Anthony?" Lamont asked. He was smugly holding the halter of a big black horse named Rebel.

"Oscar's being a bad boy," Tony said. "Now come on, Oscar. I'm new at this. Give me a break, would you?" He took a careful step. Oscar stood still. Tony took two more steps. Oscar didn't move. Holding his breath, Tony took one more step and stroked Oscar's neck.

"There we go, boy, this isn't so bad is it?" Oscar continued chewing grass. But when Tony reached for the halter, the horse tossed his head and ran away.

By this time Rick had returned. In a moment he corralled Lady. "Oscar can be kind of difficult," he said. "Why don't you try Dusty? She's pretty good-natured."

Dusty was a big brown horse, much larger than Oscar. Tony moved in warily like a thief sneaking through a hallway. To his relief, Dusty paid no attention to him. She let him rub her neck and made no move to turn away when he reached for the halter. Careful to keep away from her teeth, Tony gingerly took the halter in his fingers.

"That a girl. Let's go." But Dusty was not going anywhere. She tossed her head, pulling free from Tony's grip, and looked at him with sad, sleepy eyes. "Hey, that was uncalled for," Tony said, taking the halter again and gripping it more tightly. "Come on, let's not play around. Look, here comes Lamont back for another horse already, and I haven't gotten any of you jokers into the barn. You're making a fool out of me. Let's go."

Dusty dug in her front legs and wouldn't move. Tony, growing frustrated, started tugging harder. "Come on, you stupid animal. Move!"

"You have such a way with animals," Lamont chortled as he escorted a docile Goldie toward the barn.

Rick finally came to Tony's rescue. "Time to go to work, Dusty," he said. He pushed her so hard on the flanks that she stepped sideways. "Bring her in now. Be firm," Rick called, giving the horse another push. That seemed to end Dusty's brief rebellion. She let Tony guide her straight into the stable and into her stall.

"Hook the halter to that tether rope on the stall," Rick called as he brought in two more horses.

Tony reluctantly went out to try his luck with another horse. This time a big, red horse named Roan offered no resistance. But Tony was painfully aware that, of the seventeen Grubstake horses in the stable, he had managed to corral only two. To his amazement and embarrassment, Oscar perked up his head and ran straight to Rick. The horse seemed eager, almost frantic to get into the barn.

"How did you do that?" Tony called.

"Just a gift I have with horses," Rick said. Then, when Lamont was not looking, he said softly, "Actually, I cheated. I've got oats in this bucket. Oscar would cross a burning desert to get a taste of these."

Shortly after the horses were settled in the stable, a group of campers showed up at the corral. Their counselor was a heavy, red-haired man called Red Dog. This was the group that planned to camp out in the ridge meadow. "Got a couple of animals who can haul freight for us?" Red Dog called.

"It so happens I have two beasts who have hardly been used all summer," Rick said. "Good as new. Lamont, Tony!"

The boys poked their heads out of the stable door.

"I was thinking more of horses," Red Dog drawled. "Unless you think those fellers there can haul a couple hundred pounds apiece."

Rick ignored him. "Bring out Socks and Petey, would you?" he called to the junior wranglers. "With the tether ropes on."

Socks and Petey were sort of the leftovers at Camp Grubstake. Tony had never seen either of them out on a trail ride. Although they were not nearly as large as the draft horses, Belle and Governor, they occasionally took over pulling the buckboard wagon across the camp. But that was about all they ever did.

Lamont got to Petey first. That was fine with Tony, who thought the strawberry-colored horse was the ugliest thing in the camp. He much preferred Socks, a black horse named for the white patches on his lower legs.

"Wrangler, I hope you're kidding," said Red Dog, when Lamont and Tony emerged with their steeds. "Those two sorry hunks of horse flesh couldn't haul a box of balloons across a room."

"Everyone contributes at Camp Grubstake," said Wrangler Rick cheerfully. "These two horses have to do something to earn their keep. Where's your gear?"

"Over at Pioneer Village," said Red Dog.

"Can we ride the horses back to the village?" one of his campers asked.

"With these two, we'll get there faster if we walk," said Red Dog.

"What do you have against Socks and Petey?" asked Tony.

"I worked with them hauling the teepee poles at the start of the summer," said Red Dog. "Now, I don't like to speak ill of a fellow miracle of creation, but the minute Socks dies, Petey will be the stupidest creature on this earth."

Tony was dying to know what the horses had done to earn such an insult from Red Dog, but the counselor refused to go into specifics. "You'll see," he warned. "If we ever get our gear up on the ridge meadow it will be a miracle."

FOUR

Flying Gear

Wrangler Rick and Red Dog needed most of an hour to load up Socks and Petey with two tents, eight sleeping bags, cooking gear, and all the boys' belongings. They tied and double-tied the towering loads, straightened them up so they balanced better on the saddles, and tightened and tied some more. With every new piece of baggage, Socks sagged further. He looked so mournful that Tony began to feel sorry for him.

"Are you sure he can carry all that?" Tony asked.

"He could carry twice this," Rick said. "He's just standing there looking pitiful to get some sympathy so he can get out of doing work."

In the end the horses' saddles were piled high. They reminded Tony of pack mules heading off to the gold mines. "Head 'em up and move 'em out! Yee haw!" called Red Dog.

Tony grabbed Socks's halter and tugged. Oh, here we go again, he thought, as Socks refused to budge.

"We'll go on ahead and choose a spot for camp," Red Dog said. "A garden slug in heavy boots could move faster than these animals." He called his troop together and they started out on the wide trail that wound steeply up to the ridge meadow.

"Be firm," said Rick. "You have to take charge around horses. Horses can sense fear. If they think you're scared of them, they'll push you around. If they think you don't know what you're doing, they won't cooperate."

If they know I'm nervous, what good is it to pretend I'm not? Tony wondered. He tried his best to hide the tremors he felt. He pulled Socks's head around and looked him straight in the eye. "Look, buddy," he said, "the faster you get your carcass moving, the sooner you get this load off. So let's go."

Grudgingly, Socks started moving, nodding his head mournfully.

"What a faker!" Rick chuckled.

Tony looked back at him, stunned. "I'm talking about Socks, not you," said Rick. "He acts like he's carrying the world. You guys lead your horses. I'll be right behind you. You let me know if you're having any problems."

Socks nudged past Petey into the lead, a move that surprised and pleased Tony. Maybe Wrangler Tony was getting the hang of this after all. He spoke with authority now: "Nice work, Socks. Keep it up. Don't slack off." Blowing and snorting, Socks obediently followed his lead.

After a short, steep climb, the trail leveled off for a stretch. The woods cleared, revealing dozens of mayapple plants sprouting up like little umbrellas. Socks had fallen into a steady pace. Despite Red Dog's comments about the horses' laziness, Socks was catching up with the campers. Tony could hear voices on the trail only a short distance ahead. He wanted to pick up the pace even further to prove the counselor wrong about these pack horses. But when he tugged at Socks the horse finally showed a flash of his old orneriness. Not wanting to ruin a good thing, Tony slowed down.

Just before the top of the ridge, the trail curved sharply and steeply. Here Tony found logs placed across the trail in widely spaced steps to cut down on erosion. He felt the hot breath of Socks's snort as the horse stepped over the first log, then another.

"Hold on a second, guys," Rick called. "Lamont, Petey's pack is coming unbalanced. We're almost there, but this last section is pretty steep. Let's make sure everything is snug. Tony, check the ropes and belts on your saddle just to be sure. Don't move until I finish with Petey so I can check it."

Tony had no trouble stopping Socks. He tried to inspect the saddle while still holding the tether, but Socks did not want to turn his head. Tony slid his grip to the very end of the tether to give the horse as much freedom as possible. Socks cooperated by turning his head enough so that Tony could reach the saddle while retaining his grip on the rope.

"One of the cook packs is slipping out a little," called Tony.

"Hang on a minute," Rick said, as he tightened the ropes around Petey's load.

Tony waited. Socks stood meekly, looking at him with his left eye. "You're behaving yourself good, aren't you, fella?" Tony said, patting the horse on the shoulder. "Red Dog doesn't know what he's talking about. Hold still just a second and maybe I can get that fixed myself." With his free hand, he pushed at the pack that was working free of the trusses.

It seemed caught on something. Tony planted his feet under the horse to get leverage for a better shove. That worked. But now one of the belts seemed a little loose. "Just one more thing, Socks," Tony said as he pulled on the belt buckle. But he found it too awkward to tighten the belt while holding the tether. In fact, the belt slipped a notch. Just as he decided it was best to wait for Rick after all, a stream gushed out from under the horse.

Before he could even think of moving his leg, warm urine soaked his foot. "Yiiiee! You dumb horse!" He stood in shock, one shoe and sock dripping wet.

Socks saw his chance. He jerked his head away, ripping the tether rope from Tony's hand. Tony lunged for the rope, but the horse dashed forward up the slope.

"Tony, grab him!" yelled Rick.

Tony raced after the horse, too stunned to even consider how he was going to catch a runaway horse. Socks galloped up the hill and into the clearing. Tony heard shouts from Red Dog's campers.

"Maybe Red Dog caught him," he thought. "Please, please."

But as he broke into the open under the wide sky, his heart sank. Socks was galloping over a grassy meadow, kicking and bucking like a rodeo bronco. Red Dog's boys stood well off to the north, near the edge of the woods where they had chosen to set up camp, pointing and laughing at the crazed horse. Red Dog's mouth hung open.

"We better help round him up!" Red Dog said, and he moved his heavy body into a slow jog. His campers followed him, shouting, laughing, and hooting.

The nightmare got worse. With a savage buck and kick, Socks snapped one of the ropes holding his load together. Suitcases and sleeping bags soared high into the air and landed in the grass. Encouraged by his success, Socks went crazy. He thrashed and twisted and kicked until every last bothersome piece of baggage flew off his back and into the tall grass.

"Oh, man," said Rick, passing Tony on the run. Tony tried to keep up with him. What he most wanted to do was crawl off in the grass and sneak out of camp, never to be heard from again. This was possibly the greatest disaster in the history of Camp Grubstake and there was no passing the blame. This had been a Tony Schmidt production from start to finish.

Catching Socks was no problem. Red Dog and Rick, with help from several boys, soon cornered the animal. Free of his burden, Socks stood perfectly still, wearing an expression of pure innocence. He even offered his tether to Wrangler Rick, as if he were eager to cooperate and had only been forced to act the way he had by the sheer incompetence of his handler.

Tony knew he was in deep trouble. Normally Lamont would not let an opportunity like this pass to tease him, but Lamont was not saying a word. He just looked at Tony the way you look at a man about to be shot by a firing squad.

Tony looked down at his soggy, dripping shoe in disgust. He glared at Socks. He had never hated anyone with the fury with which he hated this stupid horse. He wanted to punch the animal right in the face.

The campers stood around for a moment, eyes still wide in wonder. Clothing, bags, and cooking gear littered the meadow, as if a cyclone had hit a rummage sale.

Red Dog stood in the middle of it all with his hands on his hips, shaking his head slowly. "Now what bug bit him in the behind? I confess, I didn't believe that horse had enough spunk in him to roll over twice in the same day. I guess he showed me."

Wrangler Rick frowned darkly, and said nothing. Tony did not look forward to explaining the disaster to him or anyone else.

Red Dog, as always, seemed completely unrattled by the experience. "Well, I thank you gentlemen for bringing up our stuff. Kind of an odd way of unloading the freight, but I guess you got it here. Spread out, boys, and see what you can find. We'll drag everything over to the campsite."

"Hey, the handle's ripped off on my bag!" shouted one boy.

Tony felt blood rush to his ears. Great! The stupid horse had probably wrecked all their stuff. The kids' parents would probably sue him. Or maybe the camp would sue him. For sure they'd kick him out of the wrangler program.

"Let me know what's been damaged," Rick said, quietly. "The camp will pay for it."

As the boys scattered through the meadow, hunting for their belongings, Tony walked up to Rick. "It's my fault. I'll pay for everything," he said. "I'm just a moron when it comes to horses."

Rick put his arm around Tony. "Hey, it was an accident. That's what we carry insurance for. Although I'll bet you a million bucks our policy carrier has never seen a claim like the one they're about to get. Here," he said, offering the tether to Tony, "you want to take the horse back down?"

"I don't want to see that horse ever again as long as I live, unless it's in a dog food can," Tony said.

"Don't feel bad," Rick said gently. "I'm not blaming you. Look, what happened here is my fault. I'm supposed to be showing you how to work with horses. I guess I assumed that my dude wranglers would already have had some experience with horses. I've been letting you learn from the horses a bit too much." He looked down at Tony's wet foot. "Socks is not exactly the best teacher. You can learn a lot from him, but you usually learn the hard way."

"If I just would have waited for you, none of this would have happened," Tony said glumly.

"Come on," Rick said. "At least you gave the campers something to talk about besides aliens. That's all those kids were yapping about all the way from the stable to Pioneer Village. Everyone's talking about strange little bald men invading the camp."

"That's my fault, too," Tony said, sourly. "Although I never said it was an alien. I never said I saw anything." He glared accusingly at Lamont, who had the sense to keep quiet.

They turned for a moment to watch the campers search through grass and carry off their findings to the campsite. Except for the boy whose bag handles had been torn, Red Dog's troop was in high spirits.

"I found your sleeping bag over here, Tom!"

"Anyone seen the first-aid kit?"

"Hey, I know what spooked that horse so bad. I bet he saw the extra-terrestrial."

"Yeah, it must have been the alien!"

Rick looked at his two wranglers. "You fellas really know how to stir up a camp. I wonder what we did for excitement around here without you."

FIVE

Blindfold

Who would like to read the next verses?" Shana asked.

"I will, I will," called Bridget. "Where are we?"

"Verse three," Shana said.

"Okay. Ummmmm, what chapter?"

"Ahem," said Shana. "Been paying close attention, have we? We're on chapter two, remember?"

"Oh, yeah," Bridget said, snapping her gum loudly. She flipped a couple of pages, cleared her throat and read, "'And I was with you in weakness and in much fear and . . .'"

"What are you doing?" said Juanita. She looked over at Bridget's Bible and sighed heavily. "Bridget, you don't even have the right book. You're in Corinthians and you're supposed to be reading Philippians."

Bridget thumbed through a few pages in both directions. "Here," said Juanita, shoving her open Bible under her friend's nose. Juanita leaned back on her hands in the grass where the group sat. She listened to the water trickle quietly out of the spring just behind her and studied the treetops swaying against the blue sky. This was really a peaceful place for a Bible study, she decided. Or it would be if Bridget would ever do anything the way she was supposed to. Why in the world had she volunteered to read if she hadn't been paying the slightest attention to where the group was?

Bridget snapped her gum and cleared her throat again. "'Do nothing from selfishness or conceit, but in humility count others better than yourselves.' Gee, what kind of Bible verse is that? I'm not going to go around saying every disgusting geek and dweeb in the world is better than me. I mean, what does that do for your self-esteem?"

Juanita knew her friend well enough to know that while some of this was probably half-serious, mostly it was Bridget talking to hear herself speak. She looked at Shana to see how she would take this. Shana was probably the least flashy of the Grubstake counselors. She was quieter and more serious and did not act as crazy as the others sometimes did. Most of the campers knew her as a star basketball player for Mount Sterling College. Juanita, who loved sports, knew all about Shana and admired her. She did not want to see her drawn into a fight with Bridget.

She need not have worried. Shana shifted her long legs under her and pondered the challenge for a moment.

Bridget did not let her think long. "I mean, take your basketball stuff. What would your coach think if you went around thinking, 'Oh, dear, everyone is better than me'?"

"Well, you can't play very well if you're scared of others or if you don't have confidence in yourself," agreed Shana. "But is that what this verse is really talking about?"

"I don't know," Bridget shrugged. She closed the Bible with a thump.

"Thanks," said Juanita. "That's my Bible you closed."

"We're about done anyway, aren't we?" Bridget asked.

"Actually, you asked a good question, Bridget," Shana said. "We really ought to see if we can answer it. Why don't you all read a few more verses to yourselves and see if you can figure out why Paul wrote what he did about 'counting others better.'"

Juanita snatched her Bible from Bridget and flipped through to find Philippians again. Now that Bridget had brought it up, she was curious about the verse. Why would God want me to think that other people are better than me?

"It says we're supposed to think about other people more than we think about ourselves," said Angie.

"Why?" persisted Shana. "Keep reading."

Juanita finally found the chapter again and struggled to catch up with the others. After a few seconds of silence, Megan said, "Because God thinks of others. And that's why he sent Jesus."

"And Jesus was always being a servant," Angie added. "Always thinking about others."

Shana nodded. "So what does that tell you about verse three and thinking that others are better than us?"

"I don't think we're supposed to think that others are better than us," Juanita said. "It sounds more like we're supposed to try to think of others more than ourselves, whether they're geeks or not."

Shana smiled. "Do you think Jesus ever thought of anyone as a geek?"

"Do you think there really are aliens from other planets?" Bridget asked. "I've read some books that practically prove it."

The rest of the girls stared at their counselor in silent amazement. "What does that have to do with the price of ducks in China?" Angie said.

"Nothing," Bridget said. That fact did not seem to bother her a bit. "But I mean have you ever seen UFOs or anything?"

"Back to the subject," said Juanita.

"This is supposed to be a Bible study," scolded Megan.

"So make it a Bible study question," Bridget insisted. "What does the Bible say about alien beings?"

Shana looked up wearily from beneath her wide-brimmed straw hat. "I really don't know, Bridget. Do we have to talk about this now?"

"Well, I'm sorry, but I can't think of much else," Bridget said. She still spoke rapidly and breezily, but Juanita sensed that she was genuinely scared. "There have been some strange things going on around this camp. I know I saw something, and I'm not the only one, and it gives me the creeps. There's something weird here in this camp, and I don't want to stay anymore."

Juanita saw clouds of anxiety cross the faces of some of the other girls. Amazing how fear spreads so quickly from one person to another, faster than fire on a dead pine tree. Juanita had been with Bridget every moment of camp and as far as she was concerned had not encountered anything close to an alien. Just that one moment of panic in the dark on the trail and she was quite certain what that had been. Yet even she felt pangs of fear listening to Bridget talk.

"Bridget, get off it," she said.

Shana started gnawing the insides of her cheeks. Finally she said, "I don't know anything about UFOs and aliens. But if you aren't comfortable here at Grubstake, maybe you and I need to talk about that. As far as the group goes, we are not quite finished with our study. So here's what I would like you to do." She took out a batch of blindfolds.

"Oh, is this, like, one of those trust walks?" Megan said.

"We did that last year," Juanita explained. She and Bridget had taken turns leading each other blindfolded around the camp. The exercise was supposed to demonstrate the feeling of absolute trust, since the walker had no idea where she was going. Since Shana was new at camp this year, Juanita thought, she probably was not aware of what went on last year.

"It is almost exactly like a trust walk," Shana said, "with one big exception. A trust walk is designed to be something the blindfolded person experiences. This time, I'm more concerned about the leader."

"What do you mean?" Juanita asked.

Shana brushed off the grass as she rose to her feet. "Remember the passage we read a few minutes ago?"

The girls were stumped for a moment, thanks to Bridget throwing them off track. But Juanita still had her Bible opened. After a quick review, she said, "Thinking of others first."

"Like they're more important than yourself," added Angie.

"Bingo," said Shana. "So this time I want the leader to pay attention to how it feels to lead around the other person, being totally responsible for the other person's safety. Then maybe we can talk about it. I think it would work out best if you paired off with someone you know the least well. Since there's an odd number of you, would you mind coming with me, Bridget?"

Bridget snapped her gum loudly. "No problem."

Juanita found herself awkwardly next to Angie, who was one of two girls in their group of seven she did not know. "You want to go first?" she asked holding up the blindfold to her.

"If I'm going first, then you're supposed to be blindfolded, aren't you?" Angie said. Juanita agreed that was right. She took off her glasses and let Angie tie the blue bandanna around her eyes. "Let's hit the road," she said. They wandered quite a ways, up a short hill, then down a steep bank to the creek.

"You're taking me across the creek?" Juanita asked.

"Relax. It's really shallow here, and there's some flat rocks that make really good stepping stones. Just take it slow," said Angie. Angie guided her carefully, but there was not quite enough room on the rocks for both of them. Juanita staggered slightly and got her toe damp before reaching the other side.

"Sorry about that," Angie said. "Here, you can get your revenge now." She untied the bandanna from Juanita. Juanita put her glasses back on to look at the surroundings. They were down on the creek bottom, near the barbed wire fence that separated Camp Grubstake from one of the neighboring farms. Two fat, brown cows looked at her from the other side of the fence, chewing their cuds. The ground was so low, Juanita could barely see the top of the horse barn off to the east.

Juanita helped Angie get the bandanna on. "First thing we'll do is see if we can climb that barbed wire fence. Just kidding." She led Angie along the creek for a short ways. Where the fence angled sharply up a wooded ridge, she brought Angie up the steep bank and across to the woods. She aimed for a large limestone rock that jutted out of the ground. "We'll just step around this tree and over to the rock. It's flat right behind the rock and there is some loose sand." She saw that the sand had been disturbed and wondered which of the other pairs of girls had wondered over this way.

Behind the rock, Juanita found a bread wrapper lying on a stretch of matted ground. "Hold on," she said. "I'm just going to pick up some litter back here. There we go. Now we head back toward camp."

She directed Angie across the pasture toward Meadow Village. Whenever they came across an obstacle, like a dip in the ground, the creek, or even a thistle, Juanita not only held Angie's hand but also put her other hand on Angie's upper arm. "You know, when you're so busy watching out for someone else, you really don't have time to think of yourself," Juanita said. "That's the point of this walk, isn't it?"

"Yeah," Angie said. "I suppose if everyone made a point to act that way, there would not be any selfishness in the world. No wars or hunger or anything."

"What in the world is going on?" Juanita said, suddenly. Far across the pasture, she could barely make out a sheriff's car parked on the dirt road into the visitors' parking lot. The weather had been so dry for the past two weeks that the car had kicked up a cloud of dust that was now floating away in the breeze.

"What is it?" Angie asked.

"I think it's the police."

"What?" Angie ripped the bandanna off her head and blinked in the sunlight. "Where?"

Juanita pointed across the pasture. Someone stepped out of the car and approached two adults. Juanita thought she saw Pat and Red Dog, but she was not quite sure. The one that might have been Red Dog was pointing back across the pasture.

"Hey, why's he pointing at us?" yelped Angie. "We didn't do anything."

"Of course not," Juanita said. "Maybe something happened over here. Or maybe he saw something out this way."

"Like what?" Angie said. She gulped and started looking feverishly around into the woods.

"Relax," Juanita said. "It's probably no big deal." But she was starting to feel a little uneasy herself.

"Bridget was saying she had an evil feeling about this place," Angie said, her voice trembling now. "There must be something going on if the police are here. I don't like this. Let's get back to camp."

"Come on, you can't believe her story about aliens," said Juanita, who nonetheless hurried her step a little. "I mean, Bridget's my friend and everything, but I was with her when she claimed this alien attacked her. It was just a noise."

"Maybe it wasn't an alien. Maybe it's an escaped convict."

Juanita felt a chill, as though the sun had just ducked behind a thick cloud. There it was again. Scary stories really were contagious. Like telling ghost stories at night and having nightmares. Juanita was disgusted with herself for feeling nervous. She found that she was absentmindedly scrunching the plastic bread wrapper in her hands.

Litter! Footprints! Matted ground! What if that place behind the rock was the convict's campsite? Juanita shot a glance over her shoulder at the rock. "This is crazy!" she said out loud. "There's probably a simple, reasonable explanation for the sheriff being here." But the blindfold walk was over. Juanita and Angie wasted no time rejoining their counselor.

"Guess what we saw," Angie said. But it was not news. One of the other pairs had seen the sheriff's car. Within minutes, all twenty-one campers at Meadow Village were constructing theories about what the sheriff was doing at Camp Grubstake.

SIX

Thrown

Tony had felt so small that he could have walked under the shade of grass blades when they had come down from the ridge the previous day. He fully expected to be thrown out of camp or kicked off the wrangler program, or at the very least sentenced to a hard night of shoveling manure out of the barn. But Wrangler Rick seemed more upset with himself than with Tony. When he gave the report about the fiasco with Socks he did not even mention Tony's part in the disaster.

"I guess I'll give it another shot," Tony said sleepily to Lamont as they approached the barn on Tuesday morning. "But I don't know if I'm going to survive a week with these stupid horses."

Lamont peered through sleep-crusted eyes. "I know I won't last the week if Rick keeps getting us up at this hour."

Despite his calm reaction to the ridge disaster, Rick was taking no more chances. He had summoned Tony and Lamont to the barn at 6:00 A.M. for special training before they were to ride out with any more campers.

"You guys will be helping me saddle up the horses this morning," Rick said, as they entered the barn. "I've already got them in their stalls. Now don't worry. I'll double-check everything before we let anyone ride. Remember, talk to the horse in a calm voice. Rub its neck. Pat it," he said, gently stroking the neck of Goldie, a small buckskin horse with a white face. "Tony, take the blanket. Put it right about here. Not in the middle but a little more to the front. Wait, wait."

Tony stopped and let Rick take the blanket. "Now what did I do wrong?"

"See how the horse's hair runs this way, toward the rear? If you try to slide the blanket up toward the neck it's going to push those hairs up and the horse is going to be uncomfortable. Always lift the blanket and bring it down from the neck so the hair under it lies flat. Try it, cowpoke."

Tony did as he was told. Man, these horses were more complicated than an automobile, he thought.

"Good job," said Rick. "Now put the saddle on the blanket. Good. Now here's the important part. We have to cinch that saddle tight, otherwise it can slip and the rider will fall off. Pull that cinch as tight as you can under the belly. And I don't need to tell you to not to get too far under the horse, do I?"

Tony winced, thinking of Socks's surprise for him on the trail yesterday. A good shoe ruined. He found the buckle and pulled hard.

"Harder than that," Rick said.

"I don't want to hurt her," Tony said.

Rick laughed. "Pretend this is Socks." Tony grinned and yanked tighter. "Now you think you got that as tight as you can?" Rick asked. Tony nodded.

Rick put his arm around Tony. "Cowpoke, you're going to have to learn that you can't trust these horses."

"I already know that!" said Tony.

"Here's what I mean. Goldie doesn't like that saddle tight. She wants it loose. So she's going to try and trick you into thinking it is tight. Soon as you put that saddle on, she's going to suck in air and make her belly as big as possible. Then, when you're done pulling it tight, she'll let out the air and wham, the saddle is loose. So you're going to have to put your knee in her side to make her let out the air. And, I don't have to tell you not to get yourself too far in under the horse, do I?" he said with a wink.

Tony blushed and pushed his knee into the horse. Sure enough her stomach seemed to shrink.

"Quick, pull it tight before she swells up again," Rick said.

Tony tugged hard and was surprised to find he could pull the leather two more notches beyond where it was. "Why that sneaky little—"

"Now the bit," Rick said. "You have to force this into the mouth. No horse is going to say, 'Yum, yum! Here's a bit!' See, they aren't fond of it. But since we haven't figured out how to install a steering wheel on a horse, we have to use them. So put the bit to the mouth. Don't be rough or mean, just firm. Keep pushing until she opens up."

Goldie kept her teeth clamped. It reminded Tony of when his brother was a baby and refused to eat a spoonful of vegetables. "She won't open up," Tony said. Socks's performance the day before had totally drained his small reservoir of confidence.

"Keep it there. Be firm, be firm," Rick insisted. At last Goldie opened up. "There you go," Rick said. "One horse open for business, eleven more to go."

By the time Tony and Lamont finished saddling and bridling the remaining horses, they heard voices across the corral. Lamont looked at his watch. "What gives? It's only 7:30. What are those guys doing out there?"

"We have a full camp this week," Rick said. "In order to get two rides in for each group, we had to assign one group a pre-breakfast ride. Listen, now. I lead all rides. Normally I like my dude wranglers to ride in back so we keep all potential problems between us. But you guys are still learning, and Red Dog is pretty good with horses, so I'm going to ask you two to ride in the middle with this group."

"Red Dog?" groaned Tony. "Why does it have to be Red Dog's boys?" As if he were not having enough trouble forgetting the shame of yesterday.

Tony found he still had some work to do in figuring out these diabolical horses. He could have sworn he had the saddles as snug as they could go, but Rick had to tighten two of them further.

Rick let Red Dog's group into the stable. The eight boys each found a horse to their liking and impatiently waited for Rick's permission to walk the horses out to the corral.

Red Dog inspected the remaining horses. "Surely you don't expect me to ride little Oscar," he said, lifting his belt over his large stomach. "You'd have the humane society on you so fast."

"Nobody's taken Big Red," Lamont offered. That was because nobody wanted Big Red. Everyone knew he was laziest horse in the camp.

"It would serve him right," said Red Dog. "But I think I'll test drive Pharaoh today."

Rats, Tony thought. Now all five of his top choices were spoken for. He settled for a little brown horse named Skeeter while Lamont grabbed Maggie's reins.

"Say, I saw you talking with the sheriff yesterday afternoon, Red Dog," Rick said, as they prepared to mount in the corral. "What was that all about?"

Red Dog never had a chance to answer, as six of his eight campers immediately jumped in to answer the question.

"We saw somebody sneaking around in the woods."

"Over by the river. He was trying to hide."

"We saw him duck into the woods down by the creek."

"It was a bald guy in a green shirt. He looked like a murderer."

"Now hold on," protested Red Dog, testing his weight in the stirrup before trying to mount. "You want to start a panic? Here are the facts and all the facts. If you hear anything else, it's not true. We did see some hairless individual in a green shirt down by the creek when we were on a hike yesterday morning. When I called to him, he sort of ducked away in the bushes. Pat thought we should mention it to the sheriff just in case there was someone they were looking for. So I reported what I saw. The sheriff thinks it was probably one of Edgar Schulter's kids from the farm. One of them has a buzz cut. Sheriff said he'd have a chat with them. We said 'thank you,' and they all lived happily ever after." With a huge grunt he launched himself up onto his horse.

"Too bad," Rick said. "I was hoping the sheriff was coming to lock up Socks."

I'll second that, Tony thought. He put his hands on the saddle horn just the way Rick had shown him and swung up into the saddle. I'm getting the hang of this now, he thought.

Rick started off down the creek trail riding his favorite horse, Roan. Skeeter tried to get into line next but Tony held him back. After four horses went by, he gave his mount a gentle kick. Skeeter dutifully settled into the line.

"Now here's a horse with a little intelligence," Tony called back to Lamont. "Not like that mush-for-brains Socks."

"You just have to show them who's boss," Lamont said. Skeeter trotted down the trail, bouncing and jolting so much that Tony was starting to get a headache.

"Don't just sit in the saddle or you're going to be too sore to sit by the middle of the week," Lamont said. "Stand up in the stirrups."

Tony took his advice. Sure enough, if he let his legs act as shock absorbers in rhythm with the horse, the ride smoothed out considerably.

"Where did you get to know so much about horses?" Tony asked.

"I have a lot of hidden talents," Lamont said. "Speaking of hidden, what did you think about that sighting Red Dog reported?"

"The guy in the green shirt?" Tony shrugged. "I thought he said it was just some farmer's kid."

"That was no kid," the boy in front of Tony broke in. "He didn't have a buzz cut. Man, he was bald and he ran like an old man."

"You know what I'm thinking?" Lamont said. "I'm thinking that's the alien you saw on the first day."

"Would you quit with the alien garbage already!" Tony said sharply. "I just saw something bright for a second that looked like it might be a face or a head. It was just a blur."

"Bald, though," Lamont said. "Remember, you said it was like a bald head."

"Could have been a branch with the bark stripped off," said Tony.

"I'll bet you saw the same guy," Lamont insisted. "I'll bet the sheriff is wrong. There is someone sneaking around Camp Grubstake. I think someone ought to investigate. He's got to be up to no good or he wouldn't be sneaking around like that, would he?"

"You might be right," Tony said. He was so enjoying the new, improved way of riding out a trot that he was not totally into the conversation.

"So are you going to talk to the sheriff?" Lamont asked.

"Me? You just don't get it, do you?" Tony said. "Read my lips. I did not see an alien or a criminal or anything like that."

The horses trotted across the pasture and splashed across the creek. They passed through the welcome shade of a pair of giant cottonwoods before turning onto a trail that ran through a sparse woods out to Rock Spring village.

Lamont's suggestion had gotten Tony thinking. For the hundredth time he tried hard to recreate exactly what he had seen. But many different pictures flashed through his mind, and he was never sure what was memory and what was imagination. I'd make a lousy witness, he thought.

While Tony was standing in the stirrups, lost in his thoughts, Skeeter suddenly stopped and dropped his head to the ground. Tony's crotch jammed into the saddle. He tried to hang onto the horn but his weight was already too far forward. He pitched forward over the horse's head into a half somersault.

Thud! Tony landed on his back so hard it knocked the wind out of him for a few seconds. Red Dog dismounted and came running up the trail, tugging his horse. "Hold up in front!" he shouted. "Man overboard!"

Tony got his wind back by the time he saw Red Dog's bushy face bending over him, but he was still woozy from the fall. "How you doing, son?" Red Dog asked.

"Okay," Tony said, struggling to sit up.

"Hold on a second. Nothing broken? Numb or anything?"

"Just a little sore," Tony said. For all he knew he could have broken every bone in his back. But embarrassment can overpower the most severe pain, and Tony was practically dying with shame.

"That was a beautiful dismount, but you didn't stick the landing," Red Dog said. "Even considering the degree of difficulty, the judges can't give you more than a 9.0."

By this time, Wrangler Rick had arrived, forehead knotted in concern. "Skeeter threw you?" he asked incredulously. "I don't understand it. That horse never threw anyone before. Are you okay enough to keep going?"

"I'm fine," said Tony, gritting his teeth against the pain. He climbed back into the saddle without looking at anyone.

Great, he thought. That just makes everything perfect. The dude wrangler can't even stay on a horse that never throws anyone. I'm the worst klutz they have ever had at this camp. Why in the world did I ever sign up for this stupid wrangler program?

Panic in the Night

Juanita crouched, clutching the basketball tight to her midsection as she stared into her opponent's face. She took a quick step to her left without picking up her pivot foot. As her opponent followed the movement, Juanita dashed to the right, dribbled around her, and laid the ball in the hoop. The move worked just the way Shana had told her it would.

"Game's over," called Shana. "Canteen break. Meet back at the village for a campfire at nine o'clock."

"She's a woman of few words," Bridget said to Juanita as their counselor caught the ball and dribbled it toward the equipment shack. They ambled over to the canteen window at the corner of the converted barn where the camp met for large-group indoor activities when it was raining.

"Why did we have to play basketball tonight?" said Bridget, pulling her sticky T-shirt away from her skin. "Yuck, now I'm all sweaty. We should have done this before swimming."

"Do you think Shana would let us take a shower after the campfire?" Juanita asked. "Maybe not. I suppose the bathroom will be too full of kids washing up and brushing their teeth."

"How can you think of taking a shower at this camp when it's dark out?" asked Bridget. "Didn't you ever see the movie *Psycho*?"

"Bridget, this is Camp Grubstake, not some seedy motel," Juanita reminded her.

"Yeah, but with alien creatures on the loose."

"Oh, come off it," Juanita started to scold. But she could not forget the image of the sheriff's car across the pasture, and the bread wrapper and footprints and matted grass across the creek. Kids were saying that even one of the counselors saw somebody trespassing.

Juanita was itching to tell someone about what she had found behind that rock. But Bridget was already so high-strung she was threatening to leave camp, even though she had been hyper for months looking forward to the chance to be around horses. The last thing Juanita wanted to do was get her excited over more evidence that some stranger was lurking out in the weeds. She had almost told Angie about her find while they were on their blindfold walk. But Juanita felt funny about letting someone else in on a secret that her best friend did not know. She would have felt like a traitor.

Juanita shuddered. There was somebody out there in the dark. With that in mind, a shower did not sound so appealing. "Ah well, it gets cool in the valley at night. We'll dry off in no time, especially by the fire."

"Yeah, and with all that smoke from the fire, we'll smell more like ashes than sweat anyway," Bridget said.

Juanita pointed to a large group of kids coming up the trail from Forest Village. "Quick, before they get there!"

They sprinted to the canteen window just in front of the horde of campers. "Orange pop, chips, ice-cream sandwich, and four bags of m&m's," Bridget ordered.

The camp helper behind the counter shook his head. "You know camp policy. Only two items per night. We serve good meals here, and we don't want our campers junking out."

Bridget stuck out her tongue at him. "Yes, warden, give me the pop and a bag of candy, then. I don't know what the big deal is, I ate all my supper." Juanita bought only a can of cola.

Before the two of them could find a place to sit down, Angie whistled them over. She was talking with the group of boys who were also staying in Meadow Village.

"Looks like you were right, Bridget," Angie said.

"About the aliens?" gasped Bridget, her eyes wide.

"Close. You said there was something creepy invading this camp. Tell them, John."

John Morgan was a big kid with blond hair parted down the middle. "You know that sheriff that was here?" he said, excitedly. "It was Red Dog's guys that called him in. They saw this guy out there in the creek bottoms. Red Dog saw him too, so it wasn't just them making it up. He was bald and had a big scar across his face. They think he was carrying a hunting knife in his boot. The sheriff thinks he's an escaped convict from the state prison. He might be a murderer hiding out here until the heat blows over."

"A murderer!" squealed Bridget. "You mean he really killed someone?"

"That's what murderers do," teased Juanita.

"You're so cute," Bridget said, shooting her a fake smile. "So what are they doing about it? Are the police looking for him? They're not going to let someone like that run loose in this camp, are they?"

John shrugged. "I don't know. I think they're trying to keep it hushed up so kids won't panic. They are probably organizing a search party now, but I suppose they'll wait until dark before they come in."

"What are they waiting for?" demanded Bridget. "There's a homicidal nut loose and they just sit back and wait! What about us? He could be around the next corner. Or any tree."

Juanita thought back again to the evidence she had found—the footprints and the bread wrapper. The enormity of it drained the blood from her head, and she felt herself starting to faint. She sat down and put her head low to the ground. What if she had stumbled on the killer's hideout? What if the killer had been there? She and Angie had been so isolated, he could have picked them off and no one would have ever known. What if he had been there, watching them from the woods, waiting, waiting for them to get a step closer?

"Are you okay?" Angie asked.

"I was just thinking about us wandering around on that blindfold walk."

"Ahh!" Angie shrieked. "I hadn't thought of that. We could have walked right into him. Oh, I can't stand this!" Tears started spilling from her eyes.

"I liked it better when they were just aliens," Juanita muttered. "Are you sure it wasn't an alien?"

"It could be," a boy named Peter Johnson exclaimed. "I was talking to Matt Pryor, and he said it was green with a bald head."

"See! And everyone thought I was nuts!" said Bridget.

John turned on Peter. "He had a green shirt, you idiot!" John scoffed. "Get your facts right. The guy was bald, wearing a green shirt, and carrying a knife."

"Well, isn't someone going to do something?" demanded Bridget. "They can't keep us here in this kind of danger." She spotted Shana. "Come on, Juanita!"

She took Juanita's hand and started after their counselor, who was emerging from the equipment shed. "Shana!" called Bridget, breathlessly. "You have to let us call home. There's an escaped murderer hiding out in the woods!"

Shana raised her eyebrows and stared with her hands on her hips. "Bridget, I thought we just settled all of this. If you want to go home, you're welcome to. But I can't let you call home crying about aliens and murderers. Your parents would wonder what was wrong with us."

"But it's true! Red Dog saw him. That's why the sheriff was here. Come on, they'll tell you." Bridget dragged Shana over to the knot of campers, and had John repeat what he knew. Juanita stared hard at Shana the whole time. The counselor looked puzzled rather than scared.

"Enough, enough," said Shana as other boys started adding extra details that they had heard about Red Dog's encounter. "You guys get back to the village for the campfire. Stay together if it makes you feel better. I'm going to walk down to the retreat center and ask Pat just what did happen with the sheriff."

"You're not going alone are you?" Bridget asked. "The sun's down, and it will be dark by the time you get back, and you'll be walking right by where I think I saw him that first night."

"The day I'm afraid to walk anywhere in Camp Grubstake is the day I leave," Shana said. "Now get back to camp and please don't go scaring people with a lot of wild rumors."

Juanita, Bridget, Angie, and the boys walked together the half mile up the valley to Meadow Village. Some of the boys acted like they were not scared, but Juanita could tell they were nervous. Their eyes darted from side to side around the valley like a driver's in downtown traffic.

When they reached the village, the girls scurried to their teepee. They intended to stay just long enough to grab jackets and flashlights. All of them wanted to hurry back to the group that was watching Jason, the boy's counselor at Meadow Village, light the fire. But no sooner did Juanita step inside the flap than she heard a shuffling sound. She yelped and stood up so suddenly in the doorway that Bridget rammed into her back.

"What's going on?" gasped Bridget.

"Yeah, what is going on?" asked Megan, seated by herself in the teepee on her sleeping bag. She poked her flashlight through her bags and then shined it along the edges of the teepee.

"Are you crazy?" Bridget said, spilling into the teepee. "How can you sit in here all by yourself?"

"What's bugging you now?" Megan asked, searching under her sleeping bag. "Has anyone seen my camera? I know I had it right here but I can't find it anywhere. I've looked all over the teepee. It was an expensive one, too. My mom is going to kill me 'cause I talked her into letting me bring it."

Juanita stared at Bridget, who gaped back with huge eyes. "Ohhhhh! Juanita, he's been here!" Bridget wailed. Paralyzed with fear, she stood biting her fingernails and shaking.

Juanita hugged her close. "Bridget, get a grip."

"Cut it out! You guys are scaring me," Megan said. "What are you talking about?"

"There's a mass murderer escaped from prison, and he's been seen in our camp. Red Dog saw him," said Angie.

"Come on," Megan started to scoff. But with Bridget seemingly close to a nervous breakdown, she stopped. "Are you serious? And you think he's got my camera?"

"I don't know," Juanita said. "Do murderers steal, too?"

"A criminal's a criminal," Angie said.

"You mean a killer was in our teepee today?" Megan squealed, her voice rising ever higher with excitement. "Right here? Going through my stuff?"

"Get your jacket and your flashlight quick," Juanita said. "Let's get down to the fire with the others."

For the first time in Camp Grubstake's campfire history, more eyes faced outward into the dark than looked into the hypnotic flames. Hardly anyone said a word. In the middle of one of the camp songs, Jason stopped singing but kept playing his guitar. Only the faintest echo of voices could be heard. Jason quit strumming and looked around the group, the orange flames reflecting in his glasses.

"You people are really basket cases tonight," he said. "Are you going to let a few wild rumors wreck your week?"

"They are not rumors!" Angie said. "Red Dog saw him."

"Quiet! What was that?" Bridget said. Indistinct noises filtered through the night, almost obscured by the crackling of burning wood.

"Someone's coming," John whispered. "Over there."

The group waited tensely. When a flashlight appeared from around the bushes, Juanita felt her heart jump. The light grew closer.

"Did I catch you in the middle of a meditation?" It was Shana, accompanied by Pat. "I've never heard this group so quiet," Shana said.

"They are wound up so tight, half of them would explode if you said 'boo,'" Jason said. "Can you shed some light on this escaped psycho that's terrorizing our camp?"

Pat stepped into the center of the ring next to the fire. "This is a prime example of how rumors can get out of hand." She took off her cap and fanned the smoke away from her. "Here are the facts. Red Dog and his campers saw someone they did not recognize down by the creek near the Schulter farm. Nobody saw him with a knife or a gun or hand grenades or whatever the latest rumor is. There are no escaped convicts anywhere near here. Is that clear? Now I hope we can go back to having a normal camp week. Are there any questions?"

Bridget piped up, but her voice still sounded small in the vast outdoors. "How do you know he's not a murderer?"

Pat sighed. Just then, a flurry of flashlights appeared from the opposite direction in which Shana and Pat had arrived. The lights were bouncing, accompanied by a collection of voices. A moment later, nine campers charged up the hill from the creek into the Meadow Village camp.

Pat turned to Jason. "Are these from your village?"

Jason shook his head. "They look like Outpost Village. Yeah, here comes Poke."

Poke trudged into the camplight, her black hair pulled back in a tight pony tail and a shy grin on her face.

"To what do we owe the pleasure of your company?" asked Jason.

"You owe it to a bald-headed serial killer," said Poke. "For some reason my campers think there's an escaped ax murderer running amok in the camp. They don't want to be isolated at the outpost tonight. They think that if they stay there tonight we'll all be slaughtered in our sleep. I don't know what anyone has to fear with me to protect them. But they wanted to come in closer to civilization tonight, so do you mind if we join up with you guys?"

Pat threw up her arms in exasperation. "This whole camp is going berserk. What do I have to do to convince you that there is nothing to fear?"

Fear was taking its toll on Juanita's nerves. Normally she was not the type of person to challenge an authority figure, especially in front of a group. But she did not like being scared and hated people thinking she was a coward. "Can't you can catch the creep and throw him in jail?" she snapped. "That would solve the problem. Why aren't the police here?"

"I can see it now," Shana said calmly from the outskirts of the group. "Nationwide manhunt for person seen on camp property." The group dissolved into a dozen loud, frantic arguments. Pat called for quiet but no one heard her. Finally she took Jason's guitar and hit a loud chord on it. The group quieted instantly.

"Thank you, that's better," Pat said. "I can see everyone is on pins and needles tonight. You know, thinking about frightening things is kind of like a rock rolling down a mountainside. Once it gets going, it just keeps picking up speed until there is no stopping it. I'll tell you what we will do. Tonight and tonight only, I will ask our support staff to come out and stay with the villages—Wrangler Rick, Miller, myself, and a few others. I hope that makes you feel safer. In the meantime, I want you to spend a little extra devotion time tonight. Let's ask God to restore some peace and harmony to our lives and to this camp."

When they finally settled into their sleeping bags, Bridget insisted on staying awake all night. "I can't help it," she whispered to Juanita. "I keep thinking there's someone out there and if I fall asleep I'll never wake up."

Juanita fluffed up her pillow. "I have a feeling I'll be up quite a while whether I want to or not," she said. "But I've never stayed up all night in my life. So let me ask you: How are you going to feel when people start nodding off one by one? Are you going to want to be the last one awake?"

"Oh, no, I didn't think of that. Okay, I'll try. But my heart is still going a mile a minute."

"Mine too," said Juanita. "But I'm also exhausted. So if I lie still long enough I think I'll sleep. Why don't you try thinking about the trail ride tomorrow? Maybe that will relax you."

"I doubt it," Bridget said.

Juanita heard Bridget snoring a while later. Thank God she's getting some sleep, she thought. How about a little for me too, God? Can you please watch over me tonight?

She stayed awake a while longer, listening to a symphony of regular breathing. It seemed like she stared into the darkness above her for hours. But suddenly Bridget was nudging her shoulder, saying something about horrible nightmares. Sunlight was shining through the teepee doorway.

Blind Horse

Tony trudged to the stable after breakfast, dreading the next encounter with his archenemies. He decided that horses were the ugliest, stupidest, meanest creatures in the world. He would be happy if he lived his entire life without ever seeing another one.

"What happened to you?" Lamont asked as Wrangler Rick met them at the door. The wrangler's eyes were bloodshot and his face was puffy. "I had to spend the night at Spring Village," he said. "Seems the whole camp is freaking out on deranged killers, and I had to go there and protect them. The kids were so wired they chattered most of the night. I'll bet I didn't get three hours of sleep."

"Sounds to me like you deserve to take the day off," Tony said, hopefully. "Cancel all trail rides."

"Can't. But you boys won't be riding today."

Lamont turned on Tony. "Thanks a lot. Because of you he doesn't trust either of us to ride the horses."

"Lay off him," Rick said. "It has nothing to do with how either of you ride. I'm loaning you out to Miller this morning to run garbage duty with Belle and Governor. This afternoon we have the rodeo. But before you find Miller—" he said, reaching into a dusty corner of the barn and pulling out a pitchfork and a shovel, "maid service for the horses. You can fill that wheelbarrow and dump it out back. Enjoy."

As Tony scooped a load of manure into the wheelbarrow, he realized just how far his hopes for the week had fallen. Here he was, relieved to be shoveling out a barn instead of having to ride a horse.

Lamont screwed up his face in disgust. "Are you sure this was in our contract?"

"Hey, I finally found something I'm good at," Tony said.

"I wouldn't consider this a career opportunity."

While Tony was sweeping up dirty straw, he bumped into an object hanging from a nail on a stall. Thinking it was just a bridle, he paid no attention at first. But it kept swinging from the nail for a while, catching his attention again. This was no bridle.

"Hey, Rick. What's a camera doing in here?" Tony asked. "Is it yours?"

"I've got more sense than to store a camera in a stable," Rick said. "Let me see it." Rick whistled as he ran his hand over the fine leather case. "This thing cost big bucks. One of the campers must have brought it along for a trail ride and left it. You want to run it up to Pat on your way to join Miller?"

An hour later, the two boys hopped up beside Miller on the buckboard. "Good morning, boys," Miller chirped. "Isn't it a beautiful morning to be up and about?"

"Not bad as mornings go," Lamont said, winking at Tony. They both knew how seriously Miller took his cheerful outlook on life.

"Not bad?" exclaimed Miller. "Why, boys, what more could you ask for? There's a beautiful blue sky with a bright sun, and the birds are singing. All the campers are having a wonderful time."

"Did you have to pull guard duty last night, too?" Lamont asked.

Miller nodded seriously. In a hushed voice he said, "They asked me to go out to Forest Village last night on account of some of the young people were a little frightened about that trespasser. I said, 'certainly.' You know, boys, I'm always happy to help out. But you know," he said, grabbing his lower back with a mournful look, "I'm not as spry as I once was. My bones are a little old for sleeping on the ground."

When they reached Forest Village, the campers were still finishing breakfast, moving at a snail's pace. Tony had never seen a group of kids looking so bleary.

"Would you boys be kind enough to pick up the trash for me?" Miller asked. "You know I'm not one to shirk my share of the load around here but, as I say, I am a bit sore this morning."

You think you're sore, Tony thought. Fall off a horse and see how sore you are. When he and Lamont finished their duty, they stood back while Miller turned the wagon around. Forest Village had been hacked out of the thickest woods in Camp Grubstake and so there was no room for a turn-around loop. "Belle, Governor," Miller called softly. The horses backed up at an angle, turning the wagon. Tony studied Governor closely. The horse never tripped or bumped into anything. How could he do that with those blind eyes? Some of those other horses with perfectly good vision could not walk through a pasture without bumping into something.

Miller clicked again and snapped the reins; the horses walked to the left. Another click and snap and they backed up once more. In three quick steps, the huge horses had pulled an about-face.

As the boys rejoined Miller on the wagon, Miller offered the reins to Tony. "Would you boys like to drive the team?"

Tony made no move to touch the reins. "I'd better not. With my luck, the horses would stampede down the ravine."

"No, don't say that! Belle and Governor are two of the finest work horses you'll ever meet. They won't go off on you."

"Don't be too sure," Tony said. "That's what they said about Skeeter, too."

"Hey, this is the acid test, Tony," said Lamont. "If you crack up these horses, then you know you aren't cut out for wrangling."

"Let's find out something we don't know," Tony said, grudgingly accepting the reins. "Okay, so how do I do this?"

"Just go easy," said Miller. "Say their names and give a little flick to the reins and they'll go. Flick them again and they'll go faster. You want them to stop or back up, you pull back and say 'Whoa, Belle, Governor.' Pull the reins in the direction you want them to go."

"Sounds very user friendly," said Lamont. "Idiot proof."

"There's no such thing with horses," said Tony.

But, sure enough, Belle and Governor did whatever he asked. The ride went so smoothly that Tony wondered if he was really driving the team or whether they knew where to go and what to do without him. "How does Governor do it?" Tony asked, as the horses lumbered along the grassy rut toward Meadow Village. "Being blind like that doesn't seem to bother him."

"He's a good worker," Miller agreed. "And he's a lucky horse. Belle takes good care of him."

"You mean she does the leading, and he takes his cue from her?"

"Why, yes, Tony. That's it exactly. Governor knows Belle won't lead him astray."

"But how can you tell that?" Tony asked. "I can't see any difference between them when they walk together. It seems like Governor is right in step with Belle, not following behind."

Miller chuckled. "Those two have been together for many years. They have a system worked out, you can believe that. Governor can tell what Belle's up to even before we see her move."

Tony felt like a king or a Roman charioteer as he stood behind the reins. Imagine him being able to control such powerful beasts—animals that could crush him with one step if they wanted! Yet all he had to do was pull slightly in one direction or another and the team would obey. Amazing!

"So these two horses are pretty good friends, huh?" Tony said.

"Oh, that they are," Miller said. "Haven't you seen them out at pasture? Always together. Standing head to toe, swishing the flies off the other with their tails."

"What would happen to Governor if something happened to Belle?" asked Tony.

Miller shook his head gravely. "I don't know, Tony. I hope when the time comes that Governor goes first. There have been a couple of occasions when the two got separated at night. I especially remember a big storm. I believe it was eight years ago. Governor got himself caught on the other side of the creek when it was rising fast with the rain and all. That horse bellowed and bellowed until Belle found him and led him out up to shelter."

"Whoa, Belle, Governor," Tony said, tugging slightly on the reins. The horses stopped instantly. "You don't even have to tie them up when you stop, do you?"

Miller chuckled again. "Heaven and earth couldn't move them once I tell them 'whoa.' Here you go, young fellow," he said, transferring the reins to Lamont. "You can take the next turn. Just wait until we get the trash aboard." He leapt down from the wagon and ran over to the waste bags.

"What about your back?" Tony asked.

"Oh, it's terrible, terrible," he said grimacing. "Never leaves me any peace."

"Then how come I can't keep up with you?" Tony muttered to himself as old Miller ran his garbage bags to the wagon.

As the team rounded the campfire and headed out to Spring Village, Tony again admired their sure-footed stepping and cooperative nature.

He felt as though he were in the presence of someone old and wise. I guess I take back what I said about horses, he thought. They can't be so bad. I just had some bad luck with them, that's all.

But later that afternoon, the old doubts and fears crept back in as he helped Wrangler Rick prepare for the rodeo. Rick was not thrilled about the event. "I know the kids look forward to it," he complained to Pat. "But you can't tell what horses are going to do, especially around a bunch of kids who don't know anything about them."

Pat glanced at Tony. Maybe she was not thinking of the ridge incident with Socks and the flying gear, but her glance certainly reminded Tony of that incident. I guess I'm a case in point, he thought.

"I'm with you there," Pat said. "I've been thinking of doing away with the rodeo. But with all this silliness going around the camp, I'd like to do it just one more week to get their attention focused on something besides escaped convicts. Keep it simple and safe."

"I'm just going to use Skeeter and Lady for the barrel relay," Rick said. "They won't hurt anyone if we keep everything under control."

His words drove another needle of shame into Tony. Yep, Skeeter couldn't hurt a fly, he thought. Unless you're Tony Schmidt. Then suddenly he's Kid Dynamite.

Rick surveyed the corral. Rough-hewn wooden fences bordered three sides of the area. A gate in the middle of this fence led toward the stable. The open end of the corral led to the trails and out into the pasture. "Lamont, Tony," Rick said. "During the rodeo I want you stand guard on the open end."

"What are we guarding?" asked Lamont.

"Probably nothing. But I don't like to take chances. I want you to stand there just in case one of the horses gets skittish and starts looking for open spaces. So spread yourselves out."

"How can two people spread themselves?" Lamont wondered out loud.

"What are we supposed to do if a horse comes at us?" Tony asked.

"Just put up your hands. Those little horses aren't going to run you over. If they see you standing there, they'll go another way," said Rick.

Lamont and Tony shrugged their shoulders and walked off to their stations. Lamont planted himself about twenty feet from Tony and crossed his arms. "I don't think this was in the manual either," he said.

The rules of the barrel relay were simple. One rider rode across the corral, went around a barrel, and came back. Then that rider got off and the next rider took a turn, and then the third. Three girls from Meadow Village challenged three boys from Forest Village. Tony recognized two of the girls from that first night. "Isn't that your girlfriend for the week?" he called with a grin when Bridget took her turn.

"Hey, yeah! What happened anyway?" Lamont said. "I haven't seen her since."

"I think she dumped you," chuckled Tony.

"We went steady for about twenty-five seconds," Lamont said. "That must be some kind of record."

Tony smiled as he folded his arms across his chest. Despite all his problems of the week, he felt like a big shot. He and Lamont were standing guard, protecting the other campers. He could not help feeling just a little bit important, and he liked the feeling.

NINE

Runaway!

I can't wait! Let me ride first," chirped Bridget. The sight of horses in the corral seemed to erase her fears about the stranger running loose around camp.

"Sure. You want to go second, Megan?" Juanita asked. Megan agreed.

Juanita did not mind running last. She loved athletics and was used to winning. The more pressure, the better she loved it.

"We get Skeeter," called Bridget.

"No, we want Skeeter!" called the boys.

"I called first!" said Bridget, rushing over to take Skeeter's bridle.

"Whoa, there!" said Rick, stepping in front of Bridget. "We're not going to have a tug-of-war over the horses. I'll flip a coin. Call it in the air, girls."

Rick spun a quarter high into the air.

"Heads," called Bridget.

"Tails," called Juanita at the same time.

Rick picked his quarter out of the dust and looked at them with a pained expression. "I'll call it, okay?" Bridget said. She called heads again. It came up tails.

"We'll never win now," Megan moaned. "Lady's not going to run very hard for us knowing we wanted Skeeter."

Bridget took Lady's face in her hands and nuzzled her cheeks. Lady was a paint horse, meaning she was three colors. She looked as though someone had splashed brown and black paint on her white hide. "We were just fooling, Lady," Bridget cooed. "We fooled them into taking the loser." She climbed into the saddle, still patting Lady's cheeks.

Rick raised his hand high and then dropped it. Skeeter and Lady dashed for the barrels. Bridget took a tight turn at the barrels and opened up a big lead on the return trip. She breezed back to the starting line and hopped down.

Megan was more timid. She took a moment to get comfortable in the saddle. By the time she tiptoed her horse around the barrels, the boys had pulled even.

Juanita was so eager to go she practically threw Megan out of the saddle. With only one foot in the stirrup, she urged Lady into a fast canter. Lady almost reached the barrels before Juanita got her other foot in the stirrup.

"Come on, Lady," Juanita said as she leaned into the turn. "We can get them!" Once around the barrels, she lit out for the finish, her long black ponytail flying behind her.

"Go Juanita!" screamed the girls.

"Go Brian!" screamed the boys.

Lady flew across the finish line just ahead of Skeeter. She was traveling so fast that she nearly crashed into the corral gate behind the finish.

Cheering and laughing, the girls from Meadow Village swarmed over the corral fence to congratulate Juanita. Wrangler Rick rode up to stop them, waving his cowboy hat at them. "Get back! You know the rules. Only riders in the corral!" he shouted angrily.

Juanita dismounted, her heart pounding.

"Wow, that was fun!" she said. "As far as I'm concerned, we could just skip the rest of camp and have a week-long rodeo."

"Thanks a lot," said Shana, who had joined the celebration party.

Juanita immediately felt bad about her remark. "I didn't mean it like that," she said. "I'm just excited. That was such a great race."

"Well, when you're through celebrating here, there's something else for Megan to celebrate," Shana said. "Go up to the camp office. There's a camera waiting for you."

"My camera! You found it!" shouted Megan.

"The killer returned it?" gasped Bridget.

Shana rested her forehead down on the corral fence for a moment. With a heavy sigh, she said, "Unless Tony Schmidt is a murderer, no. He found it in the stable. Hanging up on a post in Godiva's stall." Megan blushed. "That's right. I brought it along to the stable last night. And I forgot all about it and never even took a picture. I'll go up and get it."

"Well, it's a relief to know he wasn't in our teepee," said Bridget.

"Bridget," warned Shana, "I'm getting awfully tired of this panic about murderers."

"Let's go," Juanita said, taking Bridget's arm. Juanita could see that Shana was reaching her boiling point on this mysterious stranger business. It was best to get Bridget away from their sleep-starved counselor before something happened.

"Where are we going?" protested Bridget. "The rodeo isn't done. I want to be around the horses."

"What horses?" scoffed Juanita. "Skeeter and Lady are the only ones out here. They're more like big, overgrown sheep. Let's go visit the real horses out in the pasture."

"Hey, I like that idea."

They circled around the corral, listening to Wrangler Rick set up a tame rodeo event for the younger campers. He hitched his personal horse, Roan, to the corral fence and brought Lady and Skeeter over to the corner of the corral. He gave the competing campers two crackers each. They were to eat the crackers, mount the horse, and then the first one who could whistle would be the winner.

"What kind of a rodeo event is that?" said Bridget. "You don't even really need the horse."

"Pretty lame," Juanita agreed. "Rick must be worried about safety. Probably doesn't want the horses moving with those little kids."

"Boring," said Bridget. "I'm glad we're not sticking around for that." They crossed the plank bridge that led over the creek to the pasture. "I wish I had some sugar to give the horses," Bridget said.

A few seconds later, they heard a crack like a magnified rifle shot.

"What was that?" Bridget asked.

Some of the campers screamed at the noise. But one scream in particular caught Juanita's ear. A terrified scream. Skeeter was galloping across the corral with a shrieking, crying girl on his back.

"Look at Skeeter! That noise must have scared him," Juanita said, pointing at the corral. The horse was bolting toward the open end of the corral.

Tony had been watching Francis, the camp cook, chug along the gravel road to the office in the camp pickup. The truck was at least twenty years old, with rust bubbling through the paint. Whenever Francis touched the accelerator, the engine rumbled like a jackhammer. These guys at camp know a lot about horses, but not much about machines,

Tony thought. He was about to comment to Lamont about what an old beater that truck was. But just as the truck chugged past the corral, the engine kicked a tremendous backfire.

Tony jumped, but not as high as many of the spectators leaning out over the corral fence. "Miserable excuse for a truck," Tony muttered as the corral erupted in screams.

Suddenly, he saw something coming at him. Skeeter at a full gallop! A little girl was clinging to the saddle horn, screaming for help. Small as Skeeter was, the girl looked so tiny that she reminded Tony of a circus monkey riding one of the show horses.

Where was Rick? Tony saw Roan tied to the corral fence. He thought he saw Rick dive under Lady's neck and dash for his horse. But before he could make sure, Skeeter was almost on him. Tony gulped hard, trying not to fight off the wave of panic that crashed down on him. Go for Lamont, he pleaded, silently. But the little horse veered straight for Tony. Tony instinctively took a step to the side.

What do I do? What do I do? he thought.

"Stop him! Stop that horse!" people were screaming.

Skeeter showed no sign of slowing down. Tony could just see the horse bowling him over and trampling him. He raised his hands. "Stop, Skeeter! Hey, Skeeter!" he croaked in a small voice that not even Lamont could have heard.

"Wave your arms!" Lamont yelled.

Tony tried. He stepped as close as he dared into the horse's path and waved his hands wildly. Skeeter was not going to stop or even steer clear of him. The horse kept coming, the girl crying and begging for help. Tony inched closer so that his shoulder was directly in the horse's path.

Skeeter did not even flinch. If he even saw Tony, he did not alter his course one bit. At the last instant, Tony pulled back his shoulder to avoid getting hit. As the horse dashed past, Tony tried to grab some part of the horse to stop him. He missed the bridle and the reins that flapped loosely across in the wind. He caught a little corner of the saddle, but it ripped free from his hand. Tony stood staring numbly as the horse ran off across the pasture toward the creek bottom, the little girl bobbing on his back.

He heard shouts, each word driving home more shame.

"Stop that horse! Somebody stop him!"

"No! He's heading for the creek bottom!"

"There's a barbed wire fence over there. Somebody stop them!"

As the terrified horse and equally terrified rider streaked across the pasture, Tony saw two girls run across the field from the stable. They raced desperately to cut off Skeeter, adding their pleas of "Stop, Skeeter! Stop!"

But they were too far away. Skeeter was already past them and starting to disappear into the creek bottom when Rick thundered past on Roan. The big horse was galloping faster than Tony had ever seen a horse move. But it was too late. Skeeter was now flying down into the bottoms. He would reach the barbed wire well before Rick could catch him, even if by some miracle the little girl managed to keep her grip on the saddle horn.

Tony slumped to his knees, fighting back his own tears, coughing at the dust that Skeeter and Roan had raised. What were the chances that a horse would bolt right into the spot where he was standing guard? A million to one? Yet it had happened, and he had not done his job. He didn't stop the horse. He had failed again, only this time some poor little girl was going to pay the price of his bumbling. Tony refused to turn around and face the crowd, convinced that everyone was pointing an accusing finger at him.

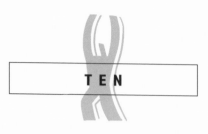

TEN

Mystery on the Creek Bottom

Juanita recognized the girl who rode past on Skeeter as Sara Palmquist, a neighbor. "Hang on Sara!" Juanita shouted, when she saw there was no hope of heading off Skeeter. Juanita looked back toward the corral and saw Roan galloping into the pasture with a cloud of dust on his tail like rocket exhaust. "Wrangler Rick's coming! Just hang on!" When Skeeter disappeared behind the brush into the bottoms, Sara was still in the saddle.

Juanita left Bridget behind. Even though she realized that she could not possibly reach Sara before Rick did, Juanita kept running as if the girl's life depended on it. She was not even sure why.

When Rick blazed past, Juanita slowed slightly. Her side hurt. She was already nearly winded, and the raised dust made it even harder to breathe. The yelling about the barbed wire fence pushed her on. Juanita prayed desperately that Sara would not get hurt, that somehow Skeeter would settle down before something awful happened.

She reached the bank that sloped down into the creek bottom. There she stopped. Her head was pounding so hard that she could not see clearly. But even when her vision cleared she could hardly believe the sight. There was Skeeter, standing and shuffling his feet next to a white stand of Queen Anne's lace. He seemed like an entirely different horse than the one who had fled the corral in wide-eyed panic.

Sara sat on his back, sobbing, but unhurt. Rick had dismounted Roan.

He was now carefully approaching Skeeter, talking gently, leading Roan by the reins.

Juanita stood deathly still, afraid that if she moved or dared breathe, the horse would take off again. When Rick grabbed Skeeter's reins, she released the air from her lungs and gasped.

She trotted down the bank, stepping around stones and thistles.

"How did you catch him so fast?" she asked.

Rick put both reins in one hand and reached out to Sara. She jumped down into his arms. As Rick set her down, he looked back at Juanita in bewilderment. "I didn't catch him," he said. "He stopped."

"You mean Skeeter just stopped by himself? She never fell off or anything?" Juanita said. Poor Sara was a mess—her nose and eyes running, racked with sobs. Juanita hugged her. Sara buried her face in Juanita's shoulder. "Are you all right, Sara? You okay now?" Juanita asked.

She nodded her head without lifting her face. Rick shrugged. "It's a miracle is all I can figure. One second that horse was running like a ghost was after him. The next, he's standing here calm as can be with her still on him."

"Thank you, God!" said Juanita, squeezing the little girl.

"That's the end of the rodeo," Rick muttered. "Forever. We dodged a bullet this time, and I'm not going to let it happen again. Look how close she came to the fence. What if Skeeter would have thrown her into it?" Juanita could see the barbs on the fence at the base of the hill separating the camp from the Schulter property. The area looked awfully familiar. Ah, this is where I took Angie on the blindfold walk, she thought.

"From now on, trail rides only," Rick said, firmly. He started up the bank, leading both horses in the direction of the trail. Then he said to Juanita, "Let's get Sara and Skeeter back to the corral."

"You are quite a rider, kid," Juanita said, taking Sara's hand. "You held on tight to that ol' Skeeter. How in the world did you get him to stop?"

"I d-don't know," Sara said. "I think somebody else did." Juanita and Rick stopped and stared at each other.

"You mean Wrangler Rick?" Juanita asked.

Sara looked totally confused. "Yeah, I think so."

"Much as I'd like to take credit," Rick said, "that horse was standing still before I reached him."

"Well, I don't know," Sara sniffled. "I was so scared I just closed my eyes and scrunched up as flat as I could go. I was scared I was going to fall off. But somebody stopped him."

Juanita scanned the creek bottom for signs of this someone else. She and Rick stared even harder at each other. "This week is just getting weirder and weirder," Rick said at last. "What makes you think someone else stopped Skeeter, Sara?"

"I don't know," she said. "I thought maybe I heard a voice. And then the horse just stopped."

"You heard a voice?" Juanita repeated.

"I think so." She started crying again. "I was scared. I don't know what happened."

"Well, never mind for now," Juanita said, putting her arm around Sara again. She studied the girl. Then she looked around toward the fence line. There was that rock where she had led Angie blindfolded. "I wonder," she said out loud.

"Just don't go carrying your wondering too far," Rick warned. "If we start letting imaginations run wild again like they did last night, we'll never get any sleep. Give Sara a chance to settle down, and maybe we'll clear it up. Man, what a weird week!"

As they emerged from the creek bottom, Bridget was the first to greet them. Other campers and staff members came running up behind her. Bridget gawked at Sara, looking for signs of injury. "Hey, the kid's all right!" she shouted. Then she hesitated. "She is all right, isn't she? I mean, she looks okay."

"She's just fine," Rick said.

"Wow!" Bridget said. "Too bad you didn't have a video camera, Juanita. I bet it was some rescue."

"I'll bet it was," Juanita answered thoughtfully.

"Three cheers for Wrangler Rick!" Bridget shouted as a crowd formed around her. Rick winced and shook his head. But everyone assumed he was just being modest and they went through with their cheer.

"I didn't do anything," Rick said sourly. "Skeeter was stopped by the time I got there."

"You mean Sara stopped Skeeter all by herself?" a camper asked. "Let's give three cheers for Sara!"

When the last cheer echoed off the ridge, Rick said, "She deserves a cheer all right. But I don't know if she stopped Skeeter, either."

Now everyone looked puzzled. "Juanita?" said Bridget.

"I didn't get here 'til after Wrangler Rick did," Juanita answered.

"You mean Skeeter just stopped?" someone asked.

"I suppose he finally came to his senses," another answered.

Sara's counselor, Kris, ran through the gathering crowd to reach Sara. "Sara, dear, are you okay? You didn't fall or anything?" Now that Sara was in good hands, Juanita left her and went over to Bridget. "Come here," Juanita said. "I need your help."

"What are you talking about?"

Juanita led her away from the crowd. "I have a hunch about what's going on, but I need to investigate. Will you come with me?"

Bridget eyed her suspiciously. "Where are we going?"

"Back out to the fence line."

Bridget glanced back at the crowd drawing away from them, heading toward the corral. "I don't want to be out by ourselves like that. Not with a killer running loose."

Juanita hesitated. She was afraid that if she told Bridget the truth, her friend would never come with her. Worse yet, she would probably throw a huge tantrum if Juanita tried to go alone. But Juanita had to admit there was a risk to her plan. It wouldn't be fair to make Bridget come along without telling her.

"I think I might know where the mystery man's hideout is."

Bridget gulped. "Well, don't tell me about it. Tell Shana or Pat or Wrangler Rick or someone. They can get the police and we'll be done with this thing and we can enjoy the rest of our week."

"I'm not sure, though," Juanita said. "It's kind of a hunch. I need to get another look at it first."

"Oh sure!" Bridget snapped, looking at Juanita as if she were insane. "You want us to snoop around all by ourselves at the killer's hideout. You've been watching too much TV. You're going to get us killed." She turned and stomped off.

"Wait. Bridget, you didn't hear what Sara said about how Skeeter stopped."

Bridget wheeled. Juanita said nothing.

"Well?" Bridget demanded.

"I won't tell you unless you come with me."

"Fine, don't tell me." She stomped off again.

"All right. She was so scared she had her eyes shut most of the time. But she thought someone else stopped the horse. She heard a voice.

Bridget, she was heading straight for that barbed wire fence and some mysterious person stopped the horse. Neither Rick nor I saw anyone else in the area. What does that suggest to you?"

"An angel," Bridget said, eyes bright with awe. "It must have been an angel."

"Okay, that's a possibility," Juanita said. "But this miracle happens to occur in the very area where I found footprints and a bread wrapper. What does that tell you?"

"That they eat bread in heaven? I don't know."

"Maybe that 'killer' hangs out here and he stopped the horse."

Bridget glared at Juanita with her hands on her hips. "You're nuts. Oh, sure, you find a bread wrapper and obviously that must be the killer's hangout. Right. There's bread wrappers at our camp. There's bread wrappers in the dump. In my garbage can at home! Wow, there are killers everywhere!"

"I know, it's pretty flimsy," Juanita said. "That's why I want to check the place again. See if there's any more evidence."

"Well, what if you're right?" Bridget asked. "What if this really is the killer's hideout? Then what in blue blazes are we doing anywhere within 100 miles of the place? Let's get out of here!"

"Because what if this person was the person who stopped Skeeter?"

"What about it?" snorted Bridget.

"Killers don't go out of their way to save people, do they? I mean, what kind of crazed murderer does that? I don't think he can be such a bad person," Juanita insisted.

"Are you willing to bet your life on it?" Bridget challenged.

When she put it that way, Juanita had second thoughts. This was probably a stupid thing to do. Maybe they should at least go and get Shana to come with them. But would Shana go along with this crazy hunch? The counselor had made it clear she had heard all the wild speculation about aliens and killers and mystery people that she cared to hear. "Bridget, somebody stopped Skeeter. If it was an angel, we won't find anything. If it was someone else, that person can't be all bad. If I don't take a look, it's going to drive me absolutely bats. Please, will you come with me?"

Bridget stood a long time, rolling her eyes. "Okay. I'll go. But only because I can't stand any more mysteries around here."

"Thanks."

They warily approached the spot where Skeeter had stopped. The dry weather had thinned out the grasses and clover and weeds and left large open patches of crusted earth. They easily found the hoof prints, so many of them that they churned the sand into a bed of powder.

"I don't think we could find any human footprints in this," Bridget said. "Even if we did, how would we know they weren't yours or Rick's? The sand is so loose, it does not make a clear print."

"You're right," Juanita said. "We need to find tracks coming from the other way, from over by the fence." She wove back and forth, probing the ground with her eyes. Still nervous about the possibility that some mysterious person was around, she glanced up frequently to make sure she was not walking into an ambush.

Bridget spent most of her time eyeing the bushes and forest and rocks. Occasionally she would poke at the ground with her foot. "Nothing here. I guess we go with the angel theory," she said.

"Wait! Look at this," Juanita said. Clearly, the ground on the far side of the Queen Anne's Lace had been disturbed. Juanita found another foot-sized depression, then another. They led toward the rock—the rock with the bread wrapper. Silently, Juanita pointed to the tracks and then to the rock at the base of the wooded hill.

"Okay, I believe you," Bridget said, breathlessly. "But I'm not going another step, and you aren't either."

Juanita bit her lip. No, she shouldn't risk it. They were out of sight from everyone else in the camp and too far for their shouts to carry. This was not safe.

"Only a fool would go any farther!" Bridget whispered.

A sharp gust of wind kicked up dust around them and whistled among the leaves of the trees on the hill. Bridget jumped at the sound. "That does it," she said. "If you want to kill yourself, you go ahead. I'm out of here." She took off running toward the corral.

Juanita's heart jumped into her throat. She was by herself. But she had to know what was behind the rock. She took a step forward. Then another. She looked down and saw another footprint. She stared at the rock, then looked back at Bridget retreating full speed up the far bank of the creek bottom and out of sight. She took one more step.

"Anyone there?" she called. The wind swept her words away. "Is someone behind that rock?"

A bolt of panic rocked her. What was she doing? What if it was an escaped murderer? What if he hadn't tried to save Sara at all? What if he had tried to grab Sara and pull her behind that rock and had run away only when he heard Rick riding up? What if that horrible psycho was lying in ambush for her behind that rock just twenty feet away? Juanita turned and fled down to the creek, crossed easily in one jump, and raced up the far side. "Bridget, wait!"

God's Punching Bag

Tony brushed the gritty sand off his jeans. He started pulling burs out of his socks as busywork to divert the shame that was seeping in. Most of the rodeo spectators ran past him into the pasture. Lamont took off with them. That was just as well, because Tony did not want to talk to anyone.

He stood watching, refusing even to pray for the girl's safety. For all God listens to me, what good would it do, he thought. She's better off if I don't say anything. A huge lump swelled in his throat. He saw his cowboy hat lying on the ground. Instead of picking it up, he stepped on it and kicked it over to the nearest corral post.

To think I looked forward to this week, he thought bitterly. One foul-up after another. Dumb stunt after dumb stunt. The butt of jokes all week. Only this latest fiasco was no laughing matter.

A scared horse had run off with a terrified little girl. Tony had been the only one in position to stop it. All week long, whenever trouble had come calling, Tony had been standing squarely at the front door. He had handled this situation the same way he had handled every other situation that had come up—like a total dope. He had only one job in the rodeo and that was to prevent a horse from dashing out of the corral. As usual, he had failed.

The only reason he lingered in the corral was to find out just how much damage his bumbling had caused. He could not turn his back on the disaster until he had totaled up the bill. He had to know exactly how great of a wimp he was. When they brought the little girl back on a stretcher, if she even came back alive, Tony would know just how much ridicule to heap on himself.

He saw the scattered campers gather around something out in the pasture. He thought he saw Roan, then Skeeter. Then he heard shouts of "Hip, hip, hooray!" He heard laughter and shouting.

She must be all right, Tony thought. Probably Rick saved her. He felt happy for the girl, but no better for himself and even resentful of Rick. If the girl escaped without damage, it was only in spite of Tony. People like Wrangler Rick were always heroes; people like Tony never were.

Tony trudged out of the corral, staring at the ground to avoid all eye contact. He masked his feelings to guard against someone trying to stop him and cheer him up. There was no more cheering up to be done. Tony Schmidt had been one of the most cheerful people in the world. In the face of earlier embarrassment and failures—and there were many—he had always kept his smile and good spirits. Good old Tony Schmidt. But now he had reached the limit. He had taken more blows than he could recover from this week. He was sick of being a loser, a failure.

Tony managed to escape the corral without encountering anyone. He walked past the retreat center to a short trail behind the registration office. The trail took him down a hill to a large, clear spring that bubbled straight out of the ground and trickled to the creek.

Tony climbed down to a smooth rock covered with dry moss. There he sat hunched over, hidden behind a box elder bush, careful to avoid a stalk of stinging nettle. The fresh smell of wintergreen clashed with the aroma of manure wafting from the corral. Even here Tony could not escape the scent of the horses that had cursed him all week.

He sat for a long time, picking off wintergreen leaves, scrunching them up and throwing them into the spring. He snapped off twigs and tossed them into the far side of the spring, watching to see how long it took the feeble current to carry the twigs into the creek.

He sat there for the rest of the afternoon and into the evening, ignoring the hollow gurgling of his empty stomach.

Finally, he heard footsteps coming down the spongy trail. Although resentful of the unwanted company, he offered no reaction. He did not even turn his head to see who was coming.

"So here you are." It was Wrangler Rick.

Tony ignored him.

"What's wrong, partner?" asked Rick, plopping down on the moss. "You didn't show up for dinner, and no one knew where you were."

"Wasn't hungry," Tony mumbled.

"Gettin' tired of horses?"

Tony shrugged.

"Horses can be the most ornery, difficult creatures sometimes," Rick said.

Tony started to agree in his mind. Then he looked out over the back field and saw Belle and Governor standing together. They were head to tail, just like Miller had said, swishing flies off each other. There weren't two creatures in the world less ornery than Belle and Governor. "Maybe it's not the horses. Maybe I'm tired of me," he said.

"Wouldn't it be nice if we could switch skins once in a while?" Rick said. "Try on someone else's." He looked at Tony sideways. "This wouldn't happen to be about that incident at the rodeo, would it?"

Tony snorted. "No. Can't think of why anything at the rodeo would upset me," he said, sarcastically.

"It is about the rodeo," Rick said. He sounded surprised. "What? You mean about Skeeter getting out of the corral?"

For the first time, Tony turned to face Rick. "You put Lamont and me out there for just that reason: to keep a horse from getting out of the corral. I didn't do it. I didn't even slow him down."

Rick nodded. "The old matador defense, huh?" When Tony looked confused, Rick added, "I had a football coach who used to rant about what he called our matador defense. You know the bullfighters? When the bull charges, they step aside and wave a blanket at them? That's what our defense was like. Not a lot of hard hitting."

Tony almost smiled at the image even though it seemed like partly an insult.

"Tony, I'm just teasing," said Rick. "It was a freak accident that scared Skeeter out of his wits. No one expected you to step in front of a crazy horse with a full head of steam. There's no reason for you to feel bad. I'm the one who let that rodeo go on in the first place. And I got caught away from my horse when Skeeter went wild. I'm the one who should feel bad. Actually, I am feeling bad now that you got me thinking about it. Thanks a lot."

Tony fought hard again to squelch a smile. "It isn't just the rodeo," he said at last. "It's all those things together. Falling in the wagon, not getting

Oscar in the barn, having Socks make a fool of me, Skeeter throwing me. Now this."

"You have had quite a week," Rick admitted.

As Tony continued he had to switch from keeping back a smile to fighting back tears. "Why does it all have to happen to me? Why can't someone else be the klutz for once? What does God have against me? I never bother anyone except for stupid stuff that happens just because I'm such a dope. Sometimes I get the feeling that whenever God needs a laugh: boom, pick on Tony Schmidt. Tony Schmidt, God's punching bag. Everyone talks about God being such a loving God. If that is true, why pick on someone like me all the time?"

Rick just listened. He made no move to speak, and so Tony rambled on. "I'm not a dude wrangler anymore. I'm not going back to the stable, except to shovel it out. That's about the only thing I'm good for. And watch, something will happen to me doing that. I don't ask much. All I want is to stay out of trouble. I don't want people looking at me and laughing and thinking what a loser I am. Why can't God find someone else to pick on?"

Tony could not believe he was saying this. He felt guiltier and dirtier for stooping to this, but he could not seem to quit. He half expected God to smite him with a thunderbolt any moment.

"That's quite a psalm you've got going," Rick said.

"What are you talking about?" Tony asked. Psalms were prayers or hymns or something like that. He wasn't in a praising mood. Rick pulled a small Bible out of his hip pocket and thumbed through it for what seemed like endless minutes. "Here, listen to Psalm 80: 'Thou dost make us the scorn of our neighbors; and our enemies laugh among themselves.' Sounds like it could have been written by Tony Schmidt."

Tony peered over Rick's shoulder at the passage.

"Hey, they get worse than that," Rick said. "That just happened to be the first one I found. If you hunt through, you'll find people who are sick and tired of God making fools out of them, and they say so."

"But what's that doing in the Bible?" asked Tony.

"What do you think happened to these people who wrote such nasty things about God in the Bible?" said Rick.

"God got mad and squashed them like bugs," Tony said.

"Ahem. Read the verse after the one I just read."

Tony took the book and read silently. "Restore us, O God of hosts; let thy face shine, that we may be saved!" He gave the book back without looking at Rick. "So?"

"This guy is madder than a wet hen about his bum luck. So mad that he wonders if God had something to do with it. And he knows God well enough that he isn't afraid to let God know what he thinks. But does he ever stop believing that God is good and will be with him?"

"I guess not," Tony said.

"Maybe that's what this psalm is doing in the Bible," said Rick, standing up. "You've got a good start on your own psalm. My question to you is, are you going to finish it?"

"Not if I have to work with horses anymore," Tony said, glumly.

Rick kicked a stone loose with his cowboy boot. "You're a page behind in the script," he said. "You've got the wrong line. You're supposed to say 'Yes, I understand everything now, thanks to your wise advice.' Go ahead, say it."

Tony could not hold back the grin this time. But he just shook his head.

"Listen, tenderfoot. You're my dude wrangler for the week, and I don't like losing my wranglers. So hang with me, okay?"

Tony shrugged.

"I'll take that as a yes. Now how about some supper?" asked Rick.

"I'm not hungry," Tony said.

"Suit yourself," said Rick. "But I missed chow time tracking you down. I'm going over to the retreat center to see if I can find some leftovers. If you aren't coming with me, then I'll leave you and Lamont in charge of the horses."

Tony looked up fearfully at him. "Don't worry," said Rick. "They're all saddled up and in their stables, and they aren't going anywhere until the evening trail ride." For the first time he noticed Tony's dirty, smashed cowboy hat. "What happened there?"

Tony twirled the hat on his finger. "Do you think that guy who wrote the psalm kicked his hat?"

"Probably kicked it all over the desert."

TWELVE

Who's in the Barn?

Tony dreaded facing Lamont, who seemed to have a comment for every situation. He could not stand any teasing right now.

Just before he reached the corral, Tony heard Lamont's voice from the parking lot. "Hey, Tony!"

Tony turned to look and saw a football spiraling silently through the air. He reached up and caught the ball at shoulder height. Lamont immediately loped toward the corral fence. Tony lofted a soft pass that led Lamont perfectly. Lamont caught the ball in stride, raised his arms in triumph, and spiked it hard. The ball bounced back at him and hit him smack in the face.

Instinctively, Tony started laughing. Lamont rubbed his face and angrily chased down the ball. "Oh yeah, I'll show you!" He climbed the fence and stood on the top rail. "Take this!" He jumped up holding the ball high with both hands. As he came down, he slammed the ball to the ground. "That will teach you to mess with me," he said.

Tony retrieved the ball and tossed it again to Lamont. "I wish I could slam dunk Socks and Skeeter," he said. He didn't know why he brought those horses up. Why invite teasing?

Lamont, though, said nothing. Tony almost thought that was worse. I must be so pathetic that he's taking pity on me, he thought. Lamont squinted down the road. "Look who's coming," he said. "Isn't that my girl-friend?"

Tony immediately recognized the horse-crazy girl and her taller friend. He reared back and heaved the football toward them. Juanita cruised under the ball and caught it effortlessly. She punted the ball back, high into the air.

"Fair catch! Fair catch!" Lamont yelled as he waved his arms wildly. He caught the ball against his chest and waited for the girls to approach. "Hey, you're pretty good with the pigskin. How about a little two-on-two?"

Bridget scowled. "I hate football. We're here to ride the horses."

Tony checked his watch. "You're early," he said. "Your group isn't supposed to be here for another half hour."

"Good," said Bridget. "Then we can spend some extra time with the horses." She immediately opened the corral gate.

"Wait a minute," Tony said, nervously. "We aren't supposed to let people mess around with the horses when Wrangler Rick isn't here."

"Oh, come on! We just want to pet them and talk to them," Bridget said, lifting the gate latch. "Especially Sheik. I'm going to adopt him. I like him better than people. Everyone thinks I'm crazy just because I have proof that there's a psycho loose in camp. Well, fine, they can all get killed; just leave me alone with the horses."

Tony looked hesitantly at Lamont, who just shrugged. Thanks a lot! Tony thought. Sure, let them go. I'm the one who always gets into trouble. He could see God's punching bag set up for another hit.

"Sorry. Rick told us not to let anyone in the stable." He walked firmly toward the gate, nudged Bridget aside, and shut the gate.

"You creep!" Bridget squawked. "Juanita, you can take this guy. Deck him!"

Tony glanced nervously at the tall, athletic-looking girl next to him. For an instant he wondered if she could take him. That would be the logical next episode in this week of horrors. Get pushed around by a girl—a younger girl, no less. But he held his ground. "You can't go in," he insisted.

Fortunately, Juanita did not have the same attitude as her friend. She seemed lost in thought, and she kept glancing across the pasture. "I can wait," she said, climbing up to sit on the corral fence.

Bridget crossed her arms and glared at both of them.

A high-pitched, nervous whinny came from the barn. Immediately, Bridget changed her tactics. "See?" she said earnestly. "They're calling us. They want us to come."

"You speak the 'horse-ish' language, do you?" Lamont cracked.

There were several more snorts and whinnies. Bridget smiled proudly at the boys. "See? They are calling us. All of them. It's unanimous. All the horses in the barn want us to come. You're supposed to be taking care of the horses, right? Well, give them what they want."

The noises from the stable puzzled Tony. He could not remember hearing anything more than a brief snort or a sigh from any of the animals all week. Now, they were all making noise. "I don't know what they want, but it sure can't be you," he said.

"Why, what's wrong with us?" Bridget snapped.

Another high-pitched whinny came from the barn. This sounded almost like a squeal. Tony and Lamont stared at each other.

"What is going on?" Lamont asked.

They heard another piercing squeal, followed by snorting and stamping and the sound of hooves banging against wood.

"Well, aren't you going to do something?" demanded Bridget.

Tony raised his eyebrows at Lamont. "I guess we better go check this out." He pushed open the gate. Immediately, Bridget dashed in ahead of him. "Hey," he started. But he could see she was not going to obey without him making a big scene, which could likely get him in as much trouble as if he let her go. Besides, he was a little nervous about this frenzied commotion in the barn. By the way Lamont was holding back, Tony could not count on him to control the situation. Bridget didn't seem to have a shy bone in her body, and she seemed to know horses. Maybe it was not such a bad idea to have her along.

As he trotted toward the stable behind her, Tony glanced back to see Lamont and Juanita following them, jogging slowly. The noise from the stable grew more intense. Several horses whinnied at once. As he drew close, not only could he hear bumping against the stall walls, but also the soft sound of hooves clopping against the dirt. The horses sounded as though they were frightened of something and were desperately trying to escape. He wondered if there was a fire, and he looked up at the sky for evidence of smoke. Nothing.

"Are you sure you want to go in there, Tony?" Lamont called. "Sounds like something is scaring them. And if a big horse is scared of it, I don't know if I want to mess with it. Maybe we should just head back and get Rick."

That made sense to Tony. But what about this pesky girl? He could not let her go in the stable. If she wouldn't stop, he couldn't. "Hey, kid, don't be dumb!" he pleaded.

Suddenly, Bridget stopped and turned, her mouth gaping in horror. "It's him! I bet it's him! The killer!"

Tony felt a jolt of fear as he stared at the stable. For a second he imagined murderous eyes staring out at him from the wide cracks in the walls. "What is all this killer talk? Come on, that's such a stupid rumor," he said.

"Oh, no, it's not!" she gasped. "We found his tracks, and his hideout and everything, and it isn't far from this stable. Juanita, I'm not going in there!"

"No one asked you to go—" said Tony exasperated. A chorus of whinnies and banging interrupted him.

"He's not a killer," Juanita said in disgust. "And listen to them! Somebody better do something." She stared hard at Tony. "If nobody else does, I'm going in there."

Tony felt a twinge of shame. This was his responsibility. Rick had left Lamont and him in charge of the horses. He looked to Lamont for help but his friend was paralyzed by indecision. "Okay," Tony said after one more fearful glance at the stable. "You girls go find Rick. He's up at the center. Go quick and get back here fast. Lamont and I will go in and see what the problem is. Hurry!"

Juanita and Bridget dashed away. With a huge sigh, Tony waved Lamont on and ran to the stable. He lifted the wooden door-jamb and pulled open the huge, creaking door. Straight-edged beams of sunlight shone down through the cracks, crisscrossing the shadows and making it difficult to see. Tony flipped on the overhead string of bulbs, casting a dim light across the barn.

Horses reared up in terror. They tossed their manes and whinnied and snorted, eyes glassy and huge. Toward the back of the barn, the horses seemed beside themselves with fear. Sheik and Roan and Maggie all strained at their tethers and kicked at their wooden stalls.

"Are you sure you want to go in?" Lamont asked.

"I'm sure I don't," Tony said. "Can you see what's bothering them?" They poked their heads in farther and tried to peer into the corners. Neither saw anything threatening.

"I guess we better take a closer look," Tony said.

Lamont nodded reluctantly. The two walked slowly into the stable in a single file, careful to stay in the center of the stable, beyond the reach of thrashing hind legs.

"Calm down! We're here. It's all right. Calm down," Lamont called in a voice that was anything but calm.

"Easy, easy," Tony said. He even ventured into a stall and put a hand on Skeeter to help settle him. "What's the matter with you guys? What's got you so upset?"

They moved through the barn, trying to settle the horses. The animals near the door responded somewhat to the boys' presence. They stopped stamping and whinnying, although they still stood rigid and shuffled their feet nervously. But the horses in the back refused to be quieted. Maggie clattered against the boards at the front of her stall as if she was trying to hide in the hay. Roan reared and pawed at his tether. Sheik gave out another high, ear-splitting cry.

Tony inched toward the three horses, hands in front of him as if to ward off whatever danger was ahead. Lamont followed at his shoulder, craning his neck to see over the stalls. As they neared the far end of the stable, Lamont ran forward and searched the last shadowed corners of the building. He turned toward Tony and shrugged, then opened the rear door to let in more light. They had walked clear through the stable without seeing anything that should have upset a horse.

"Well, what's gotten into them?" Tony asked, as the three horses continued to thrash in terror.

"Horses aren't afraid of spiders, are they?" Lamont asked. "Or mice? I mean, there's probably lots of both in here. But then it's not like they just got here. I mean, why would that give them the willies now?"

Tony shook his head, still scanning the barn in search of something dangerous. "I don't know. I hope Rick gets here soon, though. Roan's going to kill himself in another minute."

"Look at Maggie's tether. She's going to pull loose!"

Tony was bewildered. He started to rest his hand against one of the center supports, when Lamont shrieked. "Tony!"

Tony jumped three inches off the ground. "What? What is it?" he gasped. Lamont looked as scared as the horses. He could only point to the post as he backed out the door. Tony turned and looked at the post for a moment, then got a second shock in as many seconds. There, right where he had been ready to put his hand, was the biggest, fattest snake he had ever seen outside a zoo! It was coiled tightly around the post. So that was what the horses were scared of!

"What are we going to do with it?" Tony asked. But Lamont had backed completely out of the barn.

"I'm not going back in," Lamont said. "I don't care what you say about me. I hate snakes."

"But the horses!" Tony said desperately. Roan and Maggie were going crazy. Sheik was in such a lather he got a front leg caught in his food trough. Tony was afraid the horses might break a leg. He knew horses that broke legs were shot, and he sure didn't want to see that happen to Sheik. Especially not during his watch.

"Kill it! Get a shovel and kill it!" called Lamont.

Blindly, Tony ran back through the barn and found a manure shovel. He raced back, holding the blade of the shovel at shoulder level. He looked at the snake. He had never seen anything more evil than those beady eyes and that darting tongue.

But as he started to jab the blade to cut the snake in half, he hesitated. This was a bull snake. Although it was huge—maybe four or five feet long—it was not poisonous. Nor was it any real threat to the horses. Bull snakes eat mice and rats and all kinds of things like that. They really are not bad animals to have around. Tony lowered the shovel. It wasn't evil. It was just a snake, trying to mind its own business, caught in a place it didn't belong. Tony didn't want to kill it if he didn't have to.

But how could he get it out of the barn? Yank it off? Shaking with fear, Tony grabbed its tail and pulled.

"Are you nuts?" called Lamont, still outside.

"It's not poisonous," Tony said, cringing as he pulled, ready to let go at an instant's notice. "It's a bull snake. I just want to get it out of here."

"Bull snakes bite, you know," Lamont said. "Get it with the shovel."

Prompted by the clattering of horses in stalls and occasional whinnies, Tony clenched his teeth and pulled just a little harder. The snake held tight. Tony could not even budge it. He pulled harder, far harder than he wanted to. What if the snake suddenly let go? Tony would fall over with the snake right on him!

Tony pulled harder.

"Are you nuts?" Lamont repeated. "What are you going to do when it lets go?"

Tony didn't know. He only knew that he did not want to kill the snake, but he had to get it off the post and out of the barn. Fast! Spreading his feet apart for support, Tony got both hands on the snake and pulled steadily, leaning backward. He held his breath for fifteen or twenty seconds, then let the air out and held the next breath.

Finally the snake let go. When Tony saw the huge snake slide off the post and coil in the air, he thought his heart would jump out of his chest. He backed out of the barn, spinning in circles so that the centrifugal force would keep the snake away from him. He spun out of the barn past a yelping Lamont, who raced for cover. At the end of one final spin he let go of the snake, like a discus thrower in the Olympics. The snake soared over the creek and far out into the pasture.

Shaking so hard he could barely stand, Tony staggered to the barn to calm the horses. Before he reached the door, however, another shriek of utter terror split the air—this time it was a human voice.

THIRTEEN

Scared Stiff!

Juanita and Bridget ran through the corral toward the stable. Wrangler Rick, slowed by his cowboy boots, trailed behind them. The air echoed with the cries of terrified horses.

"I've had enough fright in one week to last me the rest of my life," Juanita said, as she kept pace with Bridget.

"No kidding! Who's idea was it to come here? Do you think the killer got those two boys?"

Juanita was about to say, "For the last time, I don't think he's a killer." She stopped herself when she realized she had already said that a dozen times that afternoon. But the more she thought about it, the more strongly she believed that the camp trespasser was not an evil killer.

As they crossed the plank bridge over the creek, they saw the back door of the stable open. "What's going on back there?" Juanita asked, pointing.

"Maybe the killer is trying to duck out the back way," Bridget said, shrinking behind Juanita. "Let Rick go first."

Juanita was about to agree, when she saw Lamont hanging on to the back door. He was flinching and backing away as if he was afraid of something. What in the world could be in there?

This time Juanita's curiosity overcame her caution. She dashed toward Lamont, leaving Bridget and Rick behind again. The creek wound close to the stable, and Juanita had to follow its winding course to the back of the barn. As she ran along the edge of the barn, she heard Lamont give out a wild cheer.

That seemed to be all the encouragement Bridget needed. "Something good happened!" she said, racing past Juanita.

Before the two girls rounded the corner to see what was going on, however, they heard a blood-curdling scream. Both froze and gaped at each other. Juanita tried hard not to even imagine what was taking place, but she kept seeing an image in her mind of blood spurting. She looked back to see if Rick was behind her. But he had not followed them. Instead, he disappeared in the front stable door.

The howling grew louder and louder, closer and closer. Had Juanita and Bridget been able to tell where the noise was coming from, they would have fled in the opposite direction. Instead they stood rooted to their spot—scared stiff!

Suddenly a bald man in a green shirt lurched around the rear door. Juanita had never seen anyone who appeared so completely insane. He was roaring and swaying from side to side. His eyes were nearly as big as Sheik's, and he had a scruffy stubble of a beard, as if he had not shaved for three or four days. He started to run straight for Bridget. So Bridget had been right after all about this homicidal stranger!

But it was a toss-up as to who was more surprised. Bridget screamed and buried her head in her hands while the man stopped as if he had run into an electric fence.

Juanita moved in to rescue her friend. She clenched her fists in case the man attacked. But the strange man merely stared for a second as the fire went out of his eyes. He approached with a slight limp.

"It's him," Bridget said in a strangled whisper. "The killer."

"I din' mean to scare you," said the man, wheezing for breath. "Honest, I weren't meanin' no harm to no one."

"Yeah, that's what they all say. Call the cops!" Juanita said. "Someone call the cops!"

Lamont and Tony gawked at them from behind the swinging door. Wrangler Rick came running out, brandishing a two-by-four in his hand. Across the corral, Shana and the rest of the girls had just arrived and were staring in open-mouthed wonder.

"Okay, fella," Rick said. "Hold it right there. Nobody move."

The man gulped and looked around like a cornered rabbit. But he did not move. "I din' mean no harm," he said sadly.

Rick moved quickly to Juanita's side. "Are you two okay?"

Juanita nodded.

"What happened?" the wrangler continued. "What's going on?"

Bridget was almost too scared to talk. "Nothing really happened, I guess," Juanita said. "This guy just kind of appeared. Screaming and everything."

"I thought he was going to kill me," Bridget whispered breathlessly. "He's the killer."

"I ain't never hurt no one," the man pleaded.

"How about you guys?" Rick called to Lamont and Tony. "Are you okay?"

"Other than getting the winkies scared out of us, fine," Lamont said.

"And the horses?" Rick asked the old man. "The stable sounded worse than a fox in a hen house. What did you do to the horses?"

"That wasn't him," Lamont said. "That was a snake." He patted Tony on the back. "My man Tony saved the day."

Rick looked confused. He turned to the bald man, who was biting on a thick lower lip with his crooked teeth. "What are you doing here?"

The man slumped his shoulders. He smelled bad, and Juanita could see his clothes were worn. "I'se just tryin' to mind my own bi'ness."

Shana ran up, her face knotted in dead seriousness. She had made her other campers stay back in the corral. "What's going on here?"

Juanita muttered in frustration. "This could take all day if people keep coming in late."

Lamont and Tony moved forward, keeping a healthy distance from the stranger. "I can explain part of it," Lamont said. "This humongous bull snake got in the barn and climbed up a post and was scaring the horses. Tony 'The Exterminator' Schmidt, here, yanked that snake off the post and heaved him clear across the creek. Right about then" he pointed to the stranger, "this guy freaks out and charges out of the bushes."

"I din' mean nothing," the man said, forlornly. "I din' wan' bother no one. But you ever get a big snake come flyin' at you outta the sky? Thought I'se gonna have a heart attack. S'prised I still got my wits."

Wrangler Rick studied him. "What are you doing in this camp in the first place?"

"He's the killer," Bridget whispered.

The man merely bowed his head and said nothing.

"I suppose we better get the sheriff," Rick said.

"No, don't," Juanita insisted, suddenly. "He's the one who stopped Skeeter. Sara might have been hurt badly if not for him."

The man looked up at her. For the first time, Juanita saw hope in those eyes. She explained about the tracks she had found in the sand by the hideaway.

"How do you know he wasn't just trying to get Sara for himself?" Bridget said, harshly.

"From his hideout he could have seen all those people chasing after Sara," answered Juanita. "I've been thinking this over. Obviously, he didn't want to be seen. Why would he risk stepping out in the open and grabbing someone? If we found Skeeter standing there without Sara, we would have turned the whole camp upside-down to find her. You know he must have barely ducked out of sight before Rick arrived. If he was a killer, he would not have taken the risk. I think he took the chance because he wanted to help Sara."

The man looked at her in wonder and scratched his whiskers. "Well, she's just a small 'un and so scared an' all, and they was comin' mighty close to the fence. Weren't much I done, but I couldn't see the child get hurt."

"So that's what happened to Skeeter!" marveled Rick.

"So why were you hiding out?" Juanita asked. Shana and Rick both stood back and kept silent. They could see the man trusted Juanita.

"I'se between jobs," the man said. "Used up all my savin's carin' for my mother. Then she went an' died an' I din' have no place to stay no more. I'se been tryin' to get work but meantime, no place to stay. Tried farm fields, but kep' gettin' chased by dogs. Me, I'se too old to run from dogs. So I says, 'there's a big church camp. No dogs there.' It's such a big place with thick woods an' all, an' I thought I could lay low 'till I found somethin'. Thought I'd find something by now, least farmhand work."

Juanita thought back to how she once wished they would just catch the trespasser and lock him up. His appearance was kind of disgusting and he smelled awful. But she wondered how many people in his position would have risked exposure by stopping Skeeter and saving Sara. And that Bible verse kept running through her mind, "In humility count others better than yourselves."

⌐

"What's your name?" she said, pleasantly.

"Henry Anderson."

"What kind of work do you do?"

He smiled shyly, showing a gumline minus a few teeth. "A little o' eve thing. Jack o' all trades, mostly. The camp wou'nt have anything the need done, I don' s'pose?"

Rick studied him seriously. "Do you know anything about auto mechanics? We've been letting a lot of things slide on equipment around here. And it almost cost us, with that backfire scaring Skeeter."

Henry nodded happily. "Done a lot of tinkerin' in my time."

Shana said, "Why don't I take Mr. Anderson over to the center and we'll talk with Pat while you go on the trail ride? Maybe do a little checking." When she saw Henry's look of hopelessness, she quickly added, "Like we would with any job applicant. You know, even if we were to take you on, we can't pay a lot. Mostly give you a chance to get back on your feet."

"I'd 'preciate it, ma'm, I surely would." Henry Anderson smoothed out his green shirt. As he joined Shana he turned back and squinted one eye at Tony.

"You wasn't aimin' that snake at me, was you?"

"Believe me, I wasn't aiming at anything," Tony said. "I just wanted to get it away from the barn as fast as possible. I'm real sorry about that."

"Tell me more about this snake business," Rick said, as they all headed into a much quieter barn than Tony had left a few minutes earlier.

Lamont did the honors, saving Tony the awkwardness of having to tell of his own heroics. A whole troop of girl campers listened intently as Lamont related the story in microscopic detail.

When he finally finished, Rick smiled at him and said, "You weren't scared of the snake, were you?"

After the glowing report Lamont had given, Tony felt strangely free. He felt no urge to put up any false fronts. "I'm still scared stiff. Shaking like a leaf," he said with a grin.

"Well, maybe we just filled two positions at this camp today," Rick said. "Mechanic and dude wrangler."

"I still don't think I'm very good around horses."

"If you care enough about them to play tug-of-war with a snake, you have the makings of a great wrangler. All you need is experience. Choose your horse, wrangler."

with pride on the trail ride. Rick actually let him ride
...ver seen anyone but Rick ride that horse. As they start-
...trail, Rick called back to him, "I want to hear the rest of
...
...hen you're done with it."
...m, Tony thought.